MY SENIOR YEAR OF AWESOME

SCHOOL DAYZ BOOK 1

Jennifer DiGiovanni

To my awesome family, Dean, Dean Christopher, Matthew, and Kristen

MY SENIOR YEAR OF AWESOME

Chapter One

Today is the beginning of the end. My last semester at Harmony High. Less than six months until graduation. Walking to school, my legs shake. My rapid breaths puff in front of me, short bursts of mini-clouds. By now, everyone knows where they're headed in the fall—everyone but me. I don't know why I can't get over my denial. My high school education is all but finished, yet I haven't applied to one college. Sure, Mom asks me what I'm doing about it. Every. Single. Day. The future looms like a swaying two-ton piano threatening to drop on my head. But I'm not ready.

I tug the zipper on my puffy, green jacket higher, slowing my pace as I travel the last block to school.

Around me, the sounds of laughter and shouting ripple through the frigid air. Two weeks off and we're all happy to be together again. For now.

I slip through clumps of students, managing to fade into the scenery. After eleven-plus years with the same group of classmates, I've perfected the art of avoiding attention. To a majority of seniors, I'm just one more person to be forgotten when we all move on to bigger and better lives outside of our small town.

As I cross through the crowded intersection, a text buzzes in from my best friend, Jana.

Jana: The votes have been counted. Meet me in front of Mrs. D's room

At Harmony High, the Senior Superlative vote is one of the few highlights of senior year.

Me: Be there in a few

I text back, then hurry up the walkway toward school.

"Hey, Sadie. Ready for mathletes practice today?" I turn to find Andy Kosolowski, who's in the running for the title of *Most Likely to Succeed*. Not only does Andy have an enormous brain, but he's also freakishly tall, with thick glasses and moppy-blond curls.

"Mathletes today?" Did I forget to check email over the break?

"Yep. Mrs. McCaffrey sent the new schedule out last night. She wants to get a jump on training before the county tournament season starts."

Darn. I was hoping to ease into my last semester. "I'll be there, I guess," I say, unable to rise to Andy's level of excitement.

"Oh, and I heard the Senior Superlatives are posted," Andy says, falling in step next to me. Wow. Mathletes and a *Most Likely to Succeed* award all in one day. Andy must be in genius heaven.

"Do you know who won?" I ask.

"Nope. On my way right now. Want to walk together?"

When he pats my shoulder, I restrain myself from shrugging away. Don't get me wrong, Andy's a nice guy, and I've known him forever. But he's not exactly the person I want standing next to me when the Senior Superlatives are announced. He's not in the running for *Best Dressed Guy* or *Guy with the Most Awesome Ride*. No, that would be someone like Dominic Altomeri.

Like an answer to my prayers, Andy's next comment is drowned out by the growl of a black Corvette Stingray rumbling down the block. Dominic's ready to kick off the second semester with style. When his window rolls down and he waves to the crowd, I raise my hand and wave back, hoping he looks my way. But, as usual, I'm not even on his radar.

Dominic whips around the corner into the student

lot, leaving me in his wake. I turn back to Andy, but now he's gone too. Breathing a small sigh of relief, I head into school.

In the senior hallway, chaos ensues. Everyone wants to know who will win the coveted awards; those voted on not by teachers or administrators, but by our high school peers. I slow my pace, letting others pass me as I search for Jana.

Truth be told, I don't expect to be chosen for an award. I'm not the funniest, smartest, or the prettiest. I'm not the crazy girl who face paints at home games. I'm Sadie Matthews, the girl who coasts through life with reasonably good grades and procrastinates all decisions away. The potentially cute (when I live up to my potential) sidekick of my super-chic best friend, Jana Rodriguez.

I turn in the direction of Mrs. Downey's room, pressing through throngs of students. Teachers patrol the hallways, ready to report anyone loitering, but this morning, like most others, seniors ignore the empty threats.

"Get to class, everyone," Principal Dailey announces over the intercom. "The Senior Superlative results will be revealed during homeroom announcements."

When I round the last corner on my way to the yearbook moderator's room, I find Jana dancing a happy hula.

"Hey, chica! Ready to see who was voted Most Fashionable?" she asks, a sing-song rhythm in her voice, her hips swiveling back and forth with each word.

Not wanting to crush Jana's dreams of greatness, I suppress my skepticism—most of it, anyway. "Do you think we actually won something?"

Jana tugs off her flip mitts and shoves them in her jacket pocket. "I thought you voted for me for Best Dressed."

"I did. Do you know if anyone else voted for you?" Thanks to the male voting bloc, the Best Dressed award usually goes to the girl in our class who pushes the limits of the school's dress code. Halter tops, uber-miniskirts, that sort of thing. Jana dresses cute, but way too conservatively.

"Let's check it out, anyway," she says.

By the time we make it to the end of the hallway, a large group has gathered around the Yearbook Committee's bulletin board. As Jana and I approach, a bunch of people turn around, all of them pointing and clapping.

"Wow, Jana. Maybe you did win Best Dressed," I say, speaking out of the side of my mouth, lest we seem overexcited.

The crowd parts to let us in, a few people now laughing outright. I glance at the board and frown when

I realize Mia Romonov has won *Best Dressed Girl*. Not a huge surprise given that she basically looks like a Russian model.

"What did you win?" I whisper to Jana. "I don't see your picture."

Jana bites on her lower lip and points to the very top of the board. "Um, Sadie, I didn't win. You did."

Smack in the center of the top row of Senior Superlatives, I spy my junior year photo, blown up to 8 x 10 size, set inside of a glittery heart. Also inside the heart is an 8 x 10 photo of Andy Kosolowski. The caption above the heart reads, "Most Likely to Get Married."

I want to die. No, I want to puke. I want to puke and then die. Andy, the biggest nerd in all of *seniordom*? The boy who wore the same Darth Vader T-shirt every day of eighth grade? The guy who passed out at middle school graduation and was trampled on by the rest of our class?

"Is this a joke?" Waves of laughter circulate around me like a bubbling, too-hot Jacuzzi. "I don't even like Andy," I say, maybe a bit too loudly. "Not at all." Eyes narrowed, I whirl around. "Who did this?"

And then Andy's tall head appears above everyone else. He scans the board and finds his picture. His mouth falls open. His eyes meet mine. A swell of laughter reignites as we stare at each other. When he cracks a small smile, I elbow my way through what feels like most of the student body to confront him.

"You fixed the vote," I say, poking him in the center of his extra-long torso.

"What? Why would I do that?" Andy looks completely confused.

"Did you think this would be funny? Like, ha-ha, let's make fun of Sadie who hasn't been on a date in … a long time." Exactly how long is personal information.

He shakes his head, acting stunned. "Maybe they mixed up my picture with someone else's." Simultaneously, we redirect our eyes to the *Most Likely to Succeed* award, posted above a photo of Cindy Min. She's ranked second in the class, albeit way behind Andy. I guess it takes more than brains to succeed.

"Listen up, people!" I shout, cupping my hands around my mouth like a megaphone. "I am so not marrying Andy Kosolowski. So ha-ha, joke's on me. Hilarious." I shoot one final look of disgust at my classmates and stomp off in the direction of homeroom.

***

I can't remember ever feeling as humiliated as I do right now. By the time I slide into my seat next to Jana, my cheeks burn from the heat of thousands of eyes focused on me.

"I don't want to talk about Senior Superlatives," I tell her. "Not one word."

Jana nods, feeling my pain. "Did you bring the book?"

Of course, with all the marry Andy nonsense, I'd nearly forgotten about the book. Every year my Aunt Tina sends me the latest version of *Fill It In,* a compilation of crucial lists to complete on one's journey toward ultimate self-awareness. It's the bible for confirmed *listoholics* like Jana and me, who spend hours debating the best type of cheese to include in a ham and cheese sandwich (Jana says good old American, and I choose sharp Provolone, but we both gave thumbs down to holey Swiss and frou-frou Brie.)

I pull the latest version of *Fill It In* from my backpack and crack the spine to loosen the pages. Jana squeals and grabs it out of my hands. She starts flipping through three hundred and sixty-five new lists, every single page offering blank lines begging for completion. *Twenty-five Strange and Random Facts about Me. Top Ten Food Cravings on Sunday Mornings. Fifteen Unique Hot Dog Toppings I Want to Try.* Stuff like that.

"I've been so waiting for this. What's today's assignment?" Jana twists away from me, prepping for the big reveal. "Ahem. Drum roll, please. *Coolest Baby Names for the 21st Century.* Dibs on girls."

At least coming up with insane celebrity-worthy child names will divert my attention from the whole Senior Superlative mess. To avoid morning announcements, I excuse myself and hide in the bathroom until the bell rings. For the rest of the morning, while everyone stares and whispers about me and my future betrothed, Jana and I devote ourselves to baby-name research, hiding our iPhones under contraptions built with tented folders and notebooks.

By the time we meet for lunch, we've each devised an alphabetical list of names and favorited our top ten.

"I like Abileen, Olivia, and Whitney," she says, dropping into the seat next to mine at our usual table. A dreamy look floats in her eyes as she imagines her future mini-me. Pretty little Abileen, with her mother's silky brown hair and coffee-colored eyes. Jana's mother is French, her father Cuban, and their genetic combination sparked my best friend's flawless complexion. Also, years of braces and faithful retainer-wearing have shaped Jana's perfect smile, which she now flashes my way, apparently satisfied with her mentally crafted reproduction.

"So, what did you come up with for your future son's name?" she asks.

"Chase."

Jana's eyes grow wide. "Chase? That's a verb, not a name."

"It's also a noun, meaning pursuit."

"Okay, Chase it is." Jana carefully scribes my top boy's name in the book. "Does Andy agree with your choice?"

I toss my empty Gatorade bottle at her head, but she ducks away, laughing.

Anyway, unlucky Chase will probably inherit my boring brown hair, a few shades short of blond, and my light brown eyes, more cafe latte compared to Jana's straight espresso. Also, I pray Chase doesn't wind up with my high forehead because boys really can't cover up that particular physical trait with fringe bangs.

"Check tomorrow's assignment." I'm more than ready to drop the subject of baby names and potential husbands. "We can start a rough draft tonight and finalize it in homeroom tomorrow."

Jana flips the page. "It's an awesome achievement list. The top ten things you've done to make your life bigger and better."

I snort into my plate of fries and ketchup. "*Fill It In* is messing with our heads. Lists are supposed to be fun."

"I know," Jana wails. "This is way too much pressure. Do you think surviving high school counts?"

"My guess is no," I say, straining to read over her shoulder.

Jana pounds the table with her fist. "We need ten solid achievements. How many do we have?"

"Um … none?"

"Senior Superlatives might count," she says.

"Not in my book." I send her a warning glare. "I can think of a million things that rank higher than a Senior Superlative."

"Really? Cause I'm blanking." She tears the page out with a decisive rrrrrrip.

"Geez-us, Jana, what are you doing?" I shriek. "That's like defacing the Holy Grail!"

"We need to keep this list with us at all times. That way, whenever the opportunity arises, we can record our achievements."

"Fine, but we can't settle for easy stuff, like passing grades. We need to do spectacular things. Things that will make history. Things that will prove Senior Superlatives mean nothing in the grand scheme of my life."

We spend the rest of lunch jotting down crazy achievements, most of which would result in expulsion or arrest. Jana keeps coming back to "falling in love" even though neither of us has any real plans for how to achieve that one.

"My mom fell in love in high school," I say, digging a plastic spoon into my yogurt. "A few months later she was pregnant and alone."

"Not every guy is your dad," Jana says, using air quotes when she speaks of the man who participated in my formation and then promptly left for college, never to return.

"High school love doesn't ever work out. So why worry about achieving it?"

"Maybe, maybe not. We'll think of something."

In my opinion, the coolest idea we come up with is riding in Dominic Altomeri's car. I've secretly been crushing on him for years. He's loud-talking but gorgeous, overconfident yet charming. Dom's also perpetually late for school, arriving every morning around the same time Principal Dailey waits by the front door with a stack of pre-printed detention notices. So, if Jana and I achieve some act of rebellion, which also results in our very first after-school time served, maybe the cosmic patterns of the universe will align, and Dominic will offer us a ride home.

"Exactly, chica! We're gonna make the most of our last few months in this horrible place," Jana says, excited by the idea of potential incarceration with one of the hottest guys in school, if only for one hour.

"Because we're either filling in ten awesome achievements and finding our soul mates or we'll be expelled and decide this was the worst idea we've ever had."

**Fill It In – Your Awesome Achievements
To Be Completed By Sadie Matthews and Jana
Rodriguez Prior to June 1st**

1.
2.
3.
4.
5.
6.
7.
8.
9.
10.

Chapter Two

Sadie and Jana's list of Sports with *Fill It In* Achievement Potential

Track and field: Coach Jenkins constantly recruits because he needs bodies to compete in the gazillion track and field events. Anyone can throw a javelin, right?

Tennis: No offense, but girls on the tennis team don't look especially athletic. Most of the time, they strut around school wearing those pleated mini-skirts. If wardrobe is a requirement for success, Jana and I could totally pull that off.

Golf: Because we're above average mini-golfers. At least if you go by those little scorecards. We're almost always close to par, and even pro golfers don't hit par all the time. Need to check if it's co-ed.

"Just pick a sport, Sadie," Jana says, handing me our list of potential activities between fifth and sixth periods. "Cause we'll probably equally suck at all of them."

"Given that tennis and golf are fall sports, and we're into January, it looks like we're running track," I say.

"Decision finalized by process of elimination," Jana agrees. "Oh, and doesn't Dominic Altomeri hold the school record in the 400 meter?"

"Is he still dating Ghouliana?" I ask. Giuliana Ryder, a junior who won last year's Miss Teen Harmony pageant, is Dom's on-and-off girlfriend, her lovely nickname perhaps due to her excessively large eyes and ghostly pale skin. But Jana and I would never be so cruel as to make fun of someone's unalterable features just because we're jealous of her ability to nab the hottest guy in town. Well, maybe once.

"I heard they broke up again over break," Jana says.

After careful observation, we conclude that Dom isn't exactly suffering from a broken heart. Admittedly, we don't hang out in the same crowd, but Jana and I notice he's had plenty of company at his lunch table, mostly of the female persuasion.

So, after watching herds of females trail Dom around school for most of the day, of course I'm shocked out of my mind when I walk into A.P. Bio and find our resident studly guy alone at a lab table.

Glancing around the room, I realize the seat next to Dom is the only one available. And sitting across the aisle from him is Andy. My tongue immediately swells to what feels like six times its normal size. At least the sudden impairment prevents any screeching mixture of horror and amazement from escaping.

I direct an uneasy glance at Jana, who's shacking up with Arlene Murphy. What the heck? My best friend sold me out for Arlene, whose anti-establishment protests include refusing to wash her hair or shave her legs.

"Welcome back, Sadie. We're switching lab partners today," Dr. Brownstein says when he notices me cowering in the doorway. A long-standing member of the ancient guard at Harmony High, he's been teaching in this very classroom since the dawn of the dinosaurs. He wears the same clothes every day—yellow rubber boots, faded jeans, and a flannel shirt, like he spent the morning mucking around in a swamp, searching for exotic reptiles.

And, truth be told, Dr. Brownstein kind of resembles a lizard, with big green eyes bugging out of his head and a tongue that flicks in and out when he speaks. The tongue thing skeeves me, which is why I avoid looking directly at his face.

"Why don't you work with Mr. Altomeri?" Dr. Brownstein asks, with a barely discernible hiss.

Well, duh. It's the only seat left. I'd never have

been late to class if I'd known about the mid-year lab partner reassignment. After hiding in bathrooms all day to avoid Senior Superlative-related pointing and staring, I'd dashed through the halls to the Science wing, leaving only seconds to spare before the bell. Seeing Andy, I briefly wonder how he's dealt with our arranged future engagement, but then I remember that most likely he had something to do with the oddly skewed results. Because I surely did not.

I take a deep breath and propel myself forward, stopping right in front of Dom. As I settle into my new seat, his dark eyes roam from my head to my toes, making me wish I'd worn something nicer than ratty jeans and a gray fleece sweatshirt. "Looks like we're stuck together." He aims a smirk in Andy's direction. "Hope your husband doesn't mind."

"Not my husband. We're nothing. He's nothing to me," I stammer, peeking at Andy as well. He's immersed in conversation with Sidh Eknath, his long-time friend. How did they manage to stay together? Seriously, you get away with so much more when you're at the top of the class. Either that or Dr. B. has no idea who our lab partners were last semester. If I hadn't been late, Jana and I might not have been separated. I turn to Jana and mouth the words, "I'm sorry." She shrugs and scoots her chair further from Arlene.

Forty-five minutes of extreme awkwardness and hormonal torture later, sweat drips down my spine, soaking the innermost layer of my sweatshirt. After three and a half years of inhaling Jana's vanilla-scented perfume, Dom's musky guy smell has me melting into a puddle of pent-up desire. Every time I look down at my paper, my overlong bangs fall forward, and I need to push them out of my line of vision in order to take proper notes. My breathing sounds abnormal, like I'm blowing air out through a tiny kazoo. Then, horror of horrors, right in the middle of Dr. Brownstein's lecture, my pen runs low on ink. When I shake it, my arm bumps Dom's elbow, sending a shock of heat through me.

I am so not washing my clothes tonight.

"Why are you writing?" Dom whispers, running a hand through his dark spiky hair, as if he fears our physical contact has disturbed his mane of perfection. "The notes are on the class website."

Red heat creeps up my neck like mercury surging in a thermometer. "I remember things better when I write them down." I set down my pen, deciding to pass on note taking for the remainder of the class.

With Dom throwing my power of concentration out of whack, I almost forget about Andy with his moppy hair, thick glasses sliding down his nose, and shoestring body with its bundle of flailing arms and legs. It's not until Dr. B. turns the lights out for a slide show that I steal a glance at the next table, wondering for the hundredth time today why a large percentage of the senior class would picture Andy and me together. It must be a huge mistake. Someone miscounted the votes. Oh, shoot, he's looking right at me.

"Hey, Sadie," he says, offering me a friendly smile. For a second, I think he's going to say something about the Senior Superlative, but he doesn't. "What'd you do over break?"

"Not much, Andy. How about you?" I aim for polite, but distant enough to discourage a longer conversation. Right now, I must seize the opportunity to captivate Dominic with my devastating wit and charm. Oh shoot, Andy's talking again.

"I went to Penn State for a physics seminar."

"Voluntarily?" I have to ask.

Andy smiles. "Yeah. Four days of Quantum Mechanics. Then I went skiing in Vermont on New Year's Day."

"And you didn't break a leg? Impressive," Dom says, while keeping his eyes glued to Dr. Brownstein's million and one pictures of amoebas.

"Can you believe what happened with the Superlatives?" Okay, Andy's going there. Why does he have to bring it up now, in front of the coolest guy who's talked to me in years? "I mean, it's not like we ever … " he shakes his head.

"It must be a mistake," I say with a short wave of my hand. "I'll swing by Mrs. Downey's room after school and sort it out." To avoid further discussion, I develop a fake obsession with single-celled creatures, crafting a glazed expression which rivals Dominic's sleeping-while-simultaneously-appearing-enthralled look. As Dr. Brownstein drones and hisses his way through class, I focus straight ahead, refusing to slide my eyes in the direction of Andy's table again, hoping he'll forget about me. Thankfully, he does.

"You are so lucky!" Jana wails, after the bell. "You get to sit between two hot guys, and I'm stuck between Arlene and the wall."

"Are you sure you looked at the right guys? Dominic is supreme hotness, but Andy is just a hot mess."

"Are we not looking at the same Andy? Cause I was thinking of moving him up from a four to a decent six or seven on our Datable Guy-O-Meter."

"A seven? Did you cut through the chem-lab on the way to class and inhale some methane?"

"C'mon, admit it. Andy's blue eyes are gorgeous. Triple-snap worthy. Potential husband worthy," Jana says, knocking her shoulder into mine as we round the corner, heading toward our lockers.

My brain clicks through a mental math exercise, silently calculating the number of days left in the school year. Way too many to stomach daily Sadie marries Andy jokes. I might need to drop out and take my GED.

"I can't really see his eyes behind his glasses," I admit.

"He wears contacts outside of school. I ran into him at the Harmony Inn once or twice, eating dinner with his family."

"Are they magical contacts that turn him into Prince Charming?"

"Like Superman when he takes off those humongous Clark Kent frames?" Jana laughs. "If Andy would bother to push a comb through his hair once in a while, he might even be an eight. Colette loves him. She's always talking about how great he is. They worked together last semester helping a bunch of mini-geniuses at the middle school with some science fair project."

I burst out laughing. "Colette loves Andy? He isn't a five on any list of mine, even if I'm seeing double and count his score twice."

"Whaaaat? You're saying Andy's a two and a half?"

"C'mon, Jana, we've known him since kindergarten. I don't even think of him as a boy, really. He's more like a blot on the wall that likes to annoy us with a bunch of dumb jokes."

"A blot who is now your future betrothed. What were

you guys talking about in class, anyway?"

"Nothing, really. He acted as if he didn't know anything about fixing the Superlative vote. Plus, he was excited about doing extra physics homework over vacation and couldn't wait to tell me about it."

Jana arches one perfectly shaped eyebrow. "Really? Why did he want to tell *you* exactly?"

I hold up my hand to block Jana's curiosity. "Don't go there. You're imagining things."

"I do have a wild imagination. But, if you don't want him, maybe you can talk him in to taking Colette to the freshman dance. She would be your friend for life."

"Oh, no. She needs to woman up and ask him herself. It's a rite of passage."

"Fine. I'll tell her to stop acting like a big baby about it. But still, be nice to Andy. I can't imagine him trying to fix the vote. He thought he was a lock for *Most Likely to Succeed*."

"And now he'll never get over the disappointment." I still can't conjure up much pity for him, though. "You know what, Jana? If Colette likes Andy so much, maybe she can walk down the aisle with him in a few years. I'll gladly surrender my supposed claim on him."

Chapter Three

After school, I cruise by the yearbook moderator's classroom to investigate the Senior Superlative voting process.

"Mrs. Downey, do you happen to have a record of the votes?" I ask after she hears my knock and ushers me inside.

She regards me from above her reading glasses. "The homeroom teachers collected the votes before winter break. We recycled the paperwork after entering everything online."

"Do you know who counted my category?" And now, I'm even more suspicious.

"May I remind you the results are confidential?" Mrs. Downey drums her fingers on her desk.

Geez, I'm not trying to undermine CIA intelligence here. I just want to know who wrote my name on a paper enough times to win a meaningless Senior Superlative vote.

Determined to find an answer, I fold my arms in front of me and remain planted in front of her desk. "I don't need to know exactly how many votes I received. I just want to know if someone possibly made an input error."

"There are thirty students on the committee," she answers, her nostrils flaring. "I've no idea who tallied each individual vote. We've never had anyone question the results before."

Great. So now I can't even use the whole 'it was a big mistake' excuse. I heave a sigh and drop my arms to my side. "Okay. Thanks, anyway."

A thin smile appears on her normally pinched face. "I'm sorry if this took you by surprise, Sadie. I understand that you and Andy aren't even dating, which is not typical of the couple voted *Most Likely to Be Married*. But, honestly, you could do much worse than be associated with Mr. Kosolowski."

"Yes, apparently Andy is quite the catch," I say, through my gritted teeth.

***

"High school is only four years. So, if we hit the jackpot and make it to one hundred, it sucks up less than five percent of our time on Earth. Why do we feel so much pressure to make these years count for something?" Jana philosophizes later that week, as we wind our way toward the cafeteria, neither of us hungry for lunch. Somehow, Jana and I always get stuck with the earliest lunch period. The sun has yet to rise above the phys ed wing, but the cafeteria ladies work at a frenetic pace, frying heaps of chicken cutlets, Thursday's featured menu item.

"According to my mom, this is the highpoint of our lives. And she spent half of senior year knocked-up."

"Oh, I really hope this isn't the best for me," Jana wails. "My happiest memories cannot revolve around vile cafeteria food at ten a.m., calculus exams, and required reading."

"What do you think we'll talk about at our fifty-year reunion?"

Jana's lips twitch into a smile. I feel an Andy joke coming on. "I picture you showing up with your husband. And Andy showing up with his wife. And the two of you laughing about being voted *Most Likely to Be Married*."

"Yeah, it will be even funnier if my husband is Dominic."

"And Andy can marry Colette."

I nod, approving Jana's vision of the future. "Sounds like a plan."

Inside the cafeteria, the smell of burnt broccoli wafts in the air, prompting us to move quickly through the lunch line.

After skipping past the cutlets and perusing today's alternate selections, we decide to split a turkey hoagie. Prison-grade lunchmeat disagrees with my stomach, but my best friend could digest rusty nails without ill effects.

We carry our trays to our usual table, and I remove three slices of carcinogen-laced turkey from my sandwich before biting into processed cheese sludge, shredded lettuce, and a mushy roll.

"I just don't see the need for us to vote on who's going to end up married," I say, after filling Jana in on my failed attempt to find answers to the Senior Superlative mystery. "This is a new millennium. We're all strong, independent young men and women. Shouldn't we focus our efforts on something important, like saving the manatees? Or discovering the true reason we were put on this planet?"

"Don't go all existential on me, chica. Everyone knows the Senior Superlative vote is the best part of high school. Besides, manatees live in the Gulf of Mexico, not the Northern Atlantic."

I scratch my fingernail over a crack in the plastic lunch tray. "Seems like we can find a better use of our collective high school brainpower than deciding who's most likely going to end up in jail or something."

Jana sets down her half hoagie, gearing up for a much-needed best friend pep talk. "Don't let it get to you. The Senior Superlative vote was a total fluke. You've never even been on one date with Andy. Have you ever held his hand at a dance or something?"

"No! Never. That's why this is all so upsetting. I'm not the type of person to campaign for votes. I didn't even think most of our classmates know my last name." I drown my sorrows in a long sip of orange Gatorade.

"Well, it doesn't look like he really believes the results either." Jana tilts her head in the direction of Geek Haven, otherwise known as Andy's lunch table. Melinda Banner, a tall sophomore with fabulous long auburn hair, is currently sitting across from my so-called better half, talking excitedly. She's pretty, in a wide-eyed, innocent sort of way, with her pale-but-no-too-pale complexion and just enough freckles to look cute, but not spotty. When Andy lifts his eyes from his PB&J to mutter a few words, she begins writing furiously in a small notebook.

"Why is she talking to him?" I ask. "She can't be … interested."

"Of course not." Jana shrugs. "She must need his help with … something."

Too weird. I turn away from Geek Haven, but still, my lunch jumps around in my stomach. "So, did you come up with any items for our awesome achievements list?"

"We should at least try out for a sport," Jana says, covering her mouth with her hand to prevent anyone from catching a glimpse of half-chewed food, one of her many odd dining habits. "If we don't make a team, we can move on to something else."

"Then, I guess we start running with wolves."

"You do mean the track team, right?"

I nod and feel my stomach dance around once more, not solely due to the aftereffects of a gross hoagie. I've never found any form of running to be enjoyable. In fact, I avoid it at all costs. Who likes sweating for no reason? But, I take solace in the fact that if I somehow survive the season, I'll be in great shape for senior week at the beach. Sporting ultra-toned abs in a bikini is a super-awesome achievement in my book.

***

According to Coach Jenkins, track is a year-round sport. So, even though the calendar just flipped to February, once Jana and I turn in our medical forms he immediately devises a daily conditioning routine for the two of us. Everyone runs in track, Coach says. Even those of us who only want to throw a javelin or attempt the long jump.

At least we're off on Thursdays, because Mrs. McCaffrey requires all mathletes to attend at least one practice each week. Also known as "The Harmony High Division of the Suburban Math League," mathletes is possibly the most cringe-worthy club in school, but moderated by the coolest teacher ever.

Toward the end of junior year, Mrs. McCaffrey sent home a conference request for my mother. I promptly lost the note in my backpack. Because everyone knows a parent-teacher meeting only happens for one of two reasons.

Reason one: You are in big, big trouble for cheating, and the teacher wants to present the evidence to your official guardian.

Reason two: Even worse, the instructor believes you are seriously mistracked and wishes to recommend that you be moved up or down to fit in with classmates at a more appropriate achievement level.

Admittedly, I wasn't 100%, beyond a reasonable doubt, sure my eyes hadn't wandered onto my neighbor's test paper during our last algebra exam. Likewise, I was 100% sure that switching classes and being without Jana would be the worst possible scenario in my high school academic life.

So, Mom never laid eyes on the note. I was home free until Mrs. McCaffrey called the night before the conference to confirm. She told Mom I was capable of advanced courses, and should not be allowed to coast through another year of geometry, like I'd planned. When Mrs. McCaffrey slid in a comment about how a large percentage of former mathletes earned scholarship money for college, I knew I was as good as dead.

At least Mrs. McCaffrey called Jana's mom the next week and delivered the same spiel about my best friend's mathematical aptitude. So, now we're both subjected to calculus and mathletes, although Jana and I found ourselves busy painting our nails on the day Mrs. McCaffrey scheduled the club's yearbook picture.

Besides Jana and me, our favorite math teacher also recruited Andy, who's not only a mathlete but the undisputed team champion. Mrs. McCaffrey even stitched a capital "C" (also the symbol for circumference if you're really geeking out) onto a baseball hat, which he proudly wears to each and every tournament.

A group of overachieving juniors and sophomores comprises the rest of our team, along with Jana's little sister Colette. Mrs. McCaffrey plucked her out of Freshman Honors Math after reviewing her high school entrance test. During matheletes practice, Colette stations herself close to Andy, as if she hopes his gifted brainwaves will penetrate her mind and further increase her cognitive abilities. She's totally hero-worshipping.

When Andy offers to help her solve some complicated theorem, Jana's little sister looks like she's on the brink of wetting her pants. Her face turns magenta, and her dark curls bob up and down as she follows Andy's step-by-step explanation.

"Ignoramus. He's toying with her," Jana whispers to me as we watch the scene from across the room.

"Jana, he's a guy."

"What does that mean?"

"He doesn't think things through enough to purposely lead her on. He treats her like his pet guinea pig because he sees her as a cute little ball of fluff following him around and trying to climb on his lap." Then Jana and I excuse ourselves for a quick bathroom trip because we're now practically peeing our pants from laughing so hard.

Once we contain ourselves and return to practice, I notice a new addition to our mathletes family. Dominic Freakin' Altomeri.

"Why are you here?" I ask, sliding back into my seat.

His expression turns sour. "McCaffrey found out I put mathletes on my app for East Carolina. They emailed her to confirm attendance. Who does that?"

My jaw drops. "You lied on a college application? Who does that?"

"Hey, take it easy on the accusations. I didn't lie. I signed up for mathletes, but with all my cross country races, I kept missing practices. Check McCaffrey's roster—my name's at the top of the list."

How did I not notice that? Come to think of it, I didn't even know an official roster existed. Geez, why don't they just make all of us wear a big nerd badge stuck to the front of our "Pi is great" t-shirts?

"So, where'd ya get in?" Dom interrupts my thoughts with the question we seniors ask each other fifty times each day. If only he knew the truth—I haven't completed one stinking application. For some reason, the thought of leaving Harmony High and entering the great unknown paralyzes me.

I fixate on the sheet of theorems Mrs. McCaffrey handed out. "Oh, I, um haven't exactly committed."

"Cool. Still thinking, huh? A girl like you must have at least ten acceptance letters." His smile sends warm shivers down my spine.

"What do you mean, a girl like me?"

"Smart. Responsible."

"Thanks, but I'm not all that."

"You take awesome notes."

"Which you must need to copy."

"Right on—I zoned out in bio today."

With a sigh, I reach into my backpack and pull out my class binder.

For the next few weeks, Dom stays after mathletes to

run for Coach Jenkins on Thursdays while Jana and I sneak out the back door and head for Starbucks. Meanwhile, Andy lingers in Mrs. McCaffrey's room for extra math practice, even though he's one of those super-intellectuals who figures out all the answers without even writing things down. Calculus actually makes sense to him. And whenever Jana and I bomb an answer, he just laughs, all "heh, heh, heh," a sound that reminds me of a creepy Muppet. But, after a few weeks of careful observation, I admit that Jana's right about Andy's slight improvement on the Datable Guy-O-Meter. In the last few years, his voice deepened a bit, and the "heh-heh" doesn't sound as Elmoish anymore. More like a hiccupping zombie on the loose, I decide. In a good way, of course.

Fill It In – February 7ᵗʰ
Ten Things To Do On A Snow Day – High School Style

1. After your mother wakes you up from a dead sleep to tell you school is cancelled, sleep in.
2. Brave blizzard conditions as you trek across town to help your best friend hide her boy band posters before the wrong person (a.k.a. Colette) steals them.
3. Binge-watch romantic vampire movies.
4. Burn through the iTunes gift cards you got for Christmas.
5. Start panicking because high school is almost over and you can't imagine being apart from your best friend when she goes to a high-class university next year on a partial scholarship.
6. Continue freaking out because you still haven't picked a college. To be honest, you haven't even submitted one application.
7. Microwave mac and cheese for a chemical-filled lunch.
8. Follow that up by devouring an entire bag of Oreos for dessert. Fact: Oreos are vegan because the creamy center contains absolutely no trace of dairy products. So, they're healthy, right?
9. After carb-loading, take a nap.
10. Pull out your empty list of awesome achievements and strategize.

Chapter Four

The Rodriguez family lives in a three-story, red brick townhouse at the end of a cobblestone street in the center of town. The entire third floor belongs to Jana because her mother's bad knee can't take two flights of stairs. As the oldest child, she also outranks Colette, their baby brother Joey (still in middle school), and Mr. Rodriguez, the guy who technically owns the place.

Jana's abundance of personal space is the reason we spend most of our free time hanging out at her house. Décor-wise, it's not the hippest spot for two high school seniors. The walls are such a vibrant pink, I'd swear a flock of flamingos exploded and spewed beta-carotene-enhanced bird parts everywhere. Frilly blankets and glitzy pillows cover her bed, but we usually push everything to the floor when we watch our favorite shows.

Friday night, we turn on a movie, but rather than zone out over a silly rom-com, we stare longingly at the empty spot on her wall where the Austin Mahone poster once hung. Jana's simultaneously packing for college and hiding stuff from her sometimes-klepto little sister. I wish I could find the desire to sort through life and move on. But, leaving my mom alone in the only apartment I've ever known feels too sad. I sense we're both avoiding the inevitable, as she hasn't pestered me about my college search since the end of winter break.

"Did you check the drama club's bulletin board lately? I think play auditions are next week," Jana says.

"Not a play. In the spring, drama club puts on a musical."

"A musical? You mean with singing? And dancing?" Jana springs up from the bed like her backside has caught fire. "We're screwed."

"Stop worrying. Anyone can do a box step. It's not like the glee club kids are so supremely talented," I insist.

"How do we prepare? Do we need to sign up ahead of time?" Jana paces the room, her long sweater flapping against the sides of her legs.

"No idea. I figured they would make a homeroom announcement or something."

Jana comes to a fast stop and folds her arms across her chest. "I'll find out, then. You're so not into this. Is it for obvious reasons?"

"Like what?" Obviously, my reasons aren't obvious to me.

"Lack of cute guys in the performing arts program?"

"Didn't Greg Spinner play the lead in Footloose two years ago? He's gorg."

"He only tried out to get publicity for his band," Jana says, plopping down in her desk chair and lifting the screen on her laptop. "He had a lot of free time after he was tossed from the baseball team for skipping practice to meet with booking agents."

"Ohhh. Is that why all those freshman girls joined the chorus?"

"Of course! They all thought they had a chance with him. Why didn't we think of that?" Jana slaps herself on the forehead, two years too late.

"Like I said, dancing and singing in front of an audience was never high on my list of things to accomplish." Not even for an amazing guitarist-athlete like Greg Spinner. I roll onto my side and peer at Jana's computer screen. "You know what, I've never even seen one of the school musicals. Why are we bothering with this?"

"Because we wanted to try new and amazing things, remember? Our list?" Jana holds up our still blank paper, which was sitting next to her laptop. I wonder if she checks it every night before bed.

"Try new things, yes. Look like an imbecile, no," I say. "Do you think we have a shot at a decent part?"

"Depends on the musical. I'm not the best singer. Okay, let me see, how do you get to drama club's page … oh, wait, *Out of Tune* is up. Well, lookee-here. Your friend Andy made the front page."

I scoot closer, squinting to read the minimized print. Lately, any sentence containing the word Andy includes my name too. The thought of headlining the school paper stops my heart mid-beat.

"Oooh, I know why Melinda was so interested in him," Jana says, pointing to the byline of the Andy article.

Most Likely to Succeed or Most Likely to Get Married? Cindy Min and Andy Kosolowski discuss the most surprising Senior Superlative vote in years.

Cindy Min, senior at Harmony High, pulled off a huge upset a few weeks ago when she was named Most Likely to Succeed over Andy Kosolowski, who's currently ranked first in the class. When I spoke with Cindy, she claimed to be just as surprised as everyone else at Harmony High. "Who knew Andy and Sadie were secretly in love? They must have tried to hide their relationship to guarantee him the Most Likely to Succeed Award. But what they say is true—love conquers all."

I need to sit up before I choke on my own saliva. Jana

reaches over to pat me on the back. We continue reading.

But this reporter investigated further. According to Andy, he is currently very much single and has never dated Sadie Matthews. "I'm just as confused as everyone," he said. So, what really happened? Was the vote sabotaged? Or does someone else out there know the real truth behind the Andy and Sadie mystery? Anonymous tips can be directed to the Out of Tune inbox. We follow up on each and every message in a timely fashion.

"Oh. My. God." I start to hiccup and taste the pizza Jana and I split for dinner.

"It's okay, chica. Andy was trying to help you out." Jana's brow furrows. "At least, I think he was."

"By bringing everything up again in the school newspaper? And what's with Melinda—why does she care so much about Andy's dating status?"

"Maybe she likes quirky guys?" Jana clicks the x on her browser to close out the page. "Okay, back to drama …"

"Right. Because my life needs more drama."

"Pfft." Jana waves her hand in front of my face. "No one reads the school paper. It's only an extra-curricular for people thinking about their future career in journalism." Jana flips down the top of her laptop and reaches for her phone. "Let's call Leslie Cooke for scoop about auditions."

Leslie has starred in every school play since our

kindergarten talent show, where she sang a memorable solo version of "Twinkle, Twinkle Little Star". Thousands of dollars' worth of voice lessons later, she belts out songs a la Kelly Clarkson, with the vocal range of Mariah Carey.

"Hi, y'all!" Leslie's honey-coated voice drips through the speaker phone. She must be working on her southern accent.

We quickly fill her in on our desire to try out for the spring musical. Jana and I are ready to fight fair and audition well. We simply want to be recognized for our natural talent. Because we're pretty sure at least one of us possesses some form of intense acting ability. We're just waiting for some big movie producer to discover our talent on YouTube.

After Jana tells Leslie about our sudden interest in drama, she responds with an ugly, hyena laugh, blasting through the speaker phone. When she regains her power of speech, Leslie informs us that Ms. Cutler, Harmony High's music teacher and spring musical director, will be staging *The Little Shop of Horrors*. Leslie plans on auditioning for the part of Audrey, but she suggests one of us would make a spectacular Audrey II. Jana assumes this means one of us will be Leslie's understudy.

"If we're the lead understudies, will that count as an awesome achievement?" Jana asks, after disconnecting the phone.

"Only if she eats too many cafeteria french fries before the show and comes down with a case of food poisoning. Then we can fill her part at the last minute," I say, knowing full well we'd never seriously hope for something so bad to happen to a friend. Or even a casual acquaintance.

"Leslie doesn't eat cafeteria food. She packs a healthy lunch. Seaweed leaves and no-salt pretzel sticks. That's why she's shaped like a toothpick," Jana says. "I guess there's a chance she may take that break a leg thing literally."

"But we would never wish bad luck on her. This list should not turn us into mean girls."

"Maybe we should rethink this achievement stuff and stick to passing Calculus," Jana says.

"After auditions. We can't give up without even trying." But I bury my face in one of Jana's fluffy pink pillows, hiding an eye twitch that fires up every time I think about singing in public.

Fill It In – Random List #1
Ten Reasons Why Sadie Matthews Will Never Pass
Her Driver's License Exam

1. I freak out when I'm behind the wheel. I have trouble remembering which button turns on the headlights. The windshield wipers swish. Then I have to cover my idiocy by pretending to see raindrops.
2. I live within walking distance of my school, a food store, and Abercrombie. Where else could I possibly need to go?
3. All my friends (except Jana) drive.
4. If I learn how to drive, I may have to look at colleges.
5. If I pass my driver's test, I can't take Driver's Ed classes anymore. And let me tell you, if you saw my instructor you would want to fail as much as possible.
6. I'm pretty sure I would somehow damage any vehicle under my control, which means I would soon be back to not driving again, anyway.
7. What would happen if I hit the accelerator instead of the brake like those senior citizens on the news, and end up in somebody's dining room? Totally awkward.
8. When going on dates, the guy should always pick up the girl at her house, according to my mom. If I can't drive, it's not even an option. Unless I go all

clandestine and walk myself to the movie theater for a secret romantic interlude.

9. If I focus too much on driving, I won't have time to help Jana complete our awesome achievements list. Which is still totally blank.

10. I can't log any practice time because Mom refuses to hand over the keys to her car until she's saved up enough money for new brakes and tires. She's been saving for three years now.

Chapter Five

The sound of a plow scraping asphalt jostles me awake. A glance out the window tells me that well over a foot of snow blanketed Harmony last night.

I maneuver around the piles of clothes, books, and college mail to retrieve my phone and unplug the charger. Cell in hand, I stretch my arms wide and try to encourage my eyes to remain open. When I hear a ding, I check for a cancellation text, but instead find a message from Jana telling me to meet her in town in an hour. Shoot. Driver's Ed is on.

I shimmy into my faded weekend jeans and a loose sweater. My apartment is dark, except for a sliver of light poking between the gap in our curtains. Mom's probably sleeping off last night's drink specials. Deciding to skip breakfast, I twist an elastic band into my unwashed hair and tug on a pair of tall boots before venturing into the frozen waves of winter slush coating the sidewalks.

Clumps of gray snow litter the roadways, kicked out from under the tires of careless drivers speeding by as if it's a warm summer day. I head for Starbucks, where Jana waits, shivering in her faux fur-trimmed parka. Even though it's an early Saturday morning, the town teems with legal-types filtering in and out of the nearby courthouse; silver-haired judges dressed in three-piece suits, young lawyers in khakis, and blue-haired document runners with nose rings, pedaling their bikes between traffic lanes.

Together, we take stock of the long coffee line, and, after a joint sigh, decide to skip our pre-Driver's-Ed lattes.

"Hate Driver's Ed," Jana grumbles. We'd both failed our permit tests (because we took them without bothering to study first) and consequently were required to sit through the school's sponsored driver's education classes. But, when it comes to studying for Driver's Ed, Jana and I follow our own academic standards.

Matthews/Rodriguez Driver's Ed Principle Number One: We refuse to study for Driver's Ed because the class is on Saturdays. Saturday! You know, the WEEKEND. Outside the government's mandated parameters for education.

Matthews/Rodriguez Driver's Ed Principle Number Two: If a class does not factor into our high school GPA we see no need to devote more than minimal brain cells to our mastery of the subject.

Matthews/Rodriguez Driver's Ed Principle Number Three: We can sit and look at pictures of cars all day long, but in no way will this teach us to become better drivers. We learn by doing.

In our opinion, driver's education is a big time waste. We need real life, on the road experience. Because we're pretty sure that after all this classroom training ends, we'll both still suck at driving.

In fact, we only bother to show up for Driver's Ed because Mr. Drum, our teacher, is kind of hot for an old guy. Ordinarily, I'm not a huge fan of former military, battle fatigue-wearing men with multiple piercings and snake tattoos. Even his eyes look Special Ops-ready, matching the greenish brown of his camo Army Ranger shirt. And I rarely wonder about what teachers do in their spare time, but Mr. Drum sparks my curiosity.

Who trades the excitement of a military career for teenage driving instruction? Was he honorably discharged or did he go AWOL and decide to hide out in Harmony? Does he crave the constant adrenaline rush associated with near-fatal accidents?

Possibly, this state of wonderment is what continually

sets off my unfortunate case of Driver's Ed amnesia. And Mr. Drum always seems to direct his attention my way whenever I'm not fully concentrating on his lecture.

"Who can tell me which vehicle has the right of way at this stop sign?" he asks, pointing to a chalk diagram sketched on the blackboard. No SMART Board for Mr. Drum—he's totally old school.

Unsurprisingly, no one volunteers.

"Miz Matthews, let's hear your perspective." Just the force of his gaze has me shrinking a few inches in my seat.

"Um …"

"Give it a try," he says.

"Okay … I guess it would be … whoever has the biggest car?"

Mr. Drum redirects his attention to the blackboard. I swear the cleft in his chin wobbles as he restrains a burst of laughter. Even his dark hair seems to shake.

"Would you further enlighten me as to your reasoning?" he finally asks, crossing his arms in front of his chest and tapping his fingers on his rock-hard bicep. He still can't look at me.

"Because you don't want to get steamrolled by a Hummer if you're only driving a Corolla?"

Sophomore guy next to me raises coughs into his fist, covering his own bout of hysterics. Newbies think Driver's Ed is all fun and games, but right now the idea of repeating this class has lost most of its humor for me.

"Interesting theory, but no." Mr. Drum clears the final echoes of restrained laughter from his throat. "I hope you never get behind the wheel of a tank. Anyone else?"

Sophomore guy's hand shoots into the air. He knows he can't possibly screw up his answer as badly as I did.

Needless to say, my post-Driver's-Ed mood is foul. Jana talks me into grabbing lunch at the indoor market located in the shell of an old textile factory a few blocks from school. Since I'm craving comfort food and my morning latte money is still in my purse, I decide to drown my sorrows in a big bread bowl of chicken noodle soup.

At the Main Street traffic light, Jana's backpack rings.

"Hold up, chica." She breaks her pace, searching for her phone buried beneath a makeup bag, our still blank achievement list, and her driving manual.

Standing in the cold, my teeth begin to chatter. "I'll go inside and find us a table." When the light changes, I step closer to the intersection.

Bam! A snowball pummels the left side of my head, spraying frozen slush into my hair.

"What the ...?" I whirl around and find Andy and his friend Sidh standing at the corner, chortling like a couple of delirious baboons.

An angry scream escapes me, echoing through the frigid atmosphere. I bend over and scoop snow with my bare hands, but when I attempt to return fire, my backpack slides down from my shoulder. The heavy bag bounces off my cheap plastic boot and a jolt of pain shoots up my leg, triggering an explosion of stars, dancing in my line of vision.

"Andrew!" I scream, stomping my uninjured foot on the ground like an irate two-year-old.

Sidh chuckles and points at Andy. "Dude, your future wife is pissed. She called you Andrew."

"She's not my future wife. Senior Superlatives are ludicrous, and I'm filing a formal appeal," Andy says, but he's laughing.

"Yeah, sure you are." Sidh flashes a toothy grin. Then his dark eyes roll side-to-side, as if he suddenly realizes he's now a target.

He's right, of course. From behind me, Jana pegs him with a snowball. But, with Jana's hand-eye coordination basically being non-existent, she might have been aiming for Andy. Her throw is wide right, and shaves Sidh's spiky-black hair above his ear, leaving him with half a head of snowy highlights.

"Got your back. But, girlfriend, you jumped about ten feet in the air." Jana laughs right along with the guys. I extract my soaking wet backpack from a pile of snow and stalk away, leaving the three of them on the far side of the street when the light changes. I hope Jana enjoys spending time with her recently elevated to datable guy status, super-nerd Andy Kosolowski.

Right now, they are all dead to me.

Two blocks later, Andy calls my name. "Sadie, I want to apologize."

I ignore him and continue power sulking.

"Sadie, stop. Please. I didn't mean to hit your head. I was aiming lower, but you're so …"

I whirl around and face him. "I'm so what?"

Andy's gaze drops to the ground as he kicks at the snow with his sneaker. "Let me make it up to you. Can I buy you a cup of coffee? Something from the bakery?"

Damn. One bad thing about going to school with the same person for approximately eleven years, five months and six days—he knows the best way to bribe me into forgiving him.

"An éclair," I snap, crossing my arms in front of my chest. "No, make it two. And a vanilla chai." With a quick nod, Andy plows through the bakery door, sending the tiny bell attached to the frame into a tinkling frenzy.

I wait five whole minutes in the cold, stomping my boots to shake off a crust of powdery snow. Eventually, Andy returns, carrying my order in a crisp, white paper bag. His glasses fogged over inside the steamy bakery, but

I still catch a glimpse of the rest of his face, twitching under the duress of holding back laughter.

Great. First, Mr. Drum, then sophomore guy, and now Andy. Nice to know I'm considered highly entertaining by the general male population.

"Ah, sorry about your hair," he says. His large hand reaches out to tuck a damp lock behind my ear.

I shake away and thrust my arm out in defense, fearing another destroy-Sadie operation is underway. "You're sorry about my hair? You bombarded my entire face with snow. I might have frostbite!"

"Nah, you're good. Your lips are still moving. Enjoy the éclairs." He hands me the bag. "Oh, and sorry about Sidh's future spouse comment. I know how much you hate the whole Senior Superlative thing."

"Yeah, I saw *Melinda's* article in the paper." I spit out the name like my mouth is filled with snake venom. Andy looks confused and opens his mouth to say something, but then decides against it. He waves good-bye and sets off in the opposite direction, whistling a happy tune, like a really tall dwarf from the Snow White fairy tale. Super-sized Dopey.

Jana passes him on her way up the street, her dark hair now tucked beneath a bright red knit cap she keeps in her backpack.

"Did Andy just buy you not one, but two éclairs?"

she asks, stunned. She grabs the bag from my hand and peeks inside, then glances at his retreating form, as if checking to make sure he's not an apparition.

"And a vanilla chai." I hoist my cup in the air.

"No freakin' way. A large chai costs at least five bucks. He could have taken you to a movie or something."

This comment has me spraying fifty cents worth of my hot beverage on the ground. Me and Andy at the movies? Together? In the dark?

"Geez-us, Jana. Do you want me to suffer third-degree mouth burns on top of everything else?"

"Sorry. He just seemed—overly concerned when you walked away."

"Unlike you, best friend."

"I thought we were joking. I didn't know you would take a little snowball so personally."

"Little? I was crushed by a flying ice bomb."

"You're absolutely right. It was a direct hit. Any lasting damage?"

"No. But don't tell Andy."

Fill It In - Random List
Ten Things I Completely Despise (okay, strongly dislike) about Andy Kosolowski

1. He thinks it's hilarious to whack defenseless young women with snowballs.

2. He's way too tall. It's disturbing.

3. His mission in life is to humiliate me. I still think he paid someone to fix the Senior Superlative vote.

4. And then after he humiliates me, he does something really nice like buying me two éclairs and a chai, knowing I can't possibly stay mad at him.

5. He's smarter than me. Okay, he's smarter than just about everyone in the universe, so this should not make me mad. But it does. And, rumor has it, he could skip school for the rest of the year and still be a lock for valedictorian.

6. He can drive.

7. He has his own car.

8. His parents probably trust him and don't ask him to leave notes whenever he goes out. I can't even walk into town alone. Hello, Mother! I'm almost eighteen.

9. He doesn't get mad. About anything. Ever.

10. He's a hair hypocrite. He tried to fix my hair after he totally wrecked it with his snowball, yet his hair always looks like he just finished wrestling a snow blower. And the snow blower won.

Chapter Six

Monday morning, I'm still mad about the snowball. And the article in the school paper. When I see Melinda in the hallway, I do an internal "Grrrrr" like an angry cat. In Calculus, I pull out my copy of *Fill It In* and fire off my list about Andy while he sits right behind me, so close I swear I can feel his raspy breath on my neck.

I know I should be capable of reaching deep into my tiny Grinch-like heart to get past his minor transgression. And he's claimed over and over that he had nothing to do with our unfortunate pairing up on the Senior Superlative board. But, possibly, he protests too much?

To be honest, I know Andy would instantly forgive me if I'd thrown a snowball in his face. He wouldn't be angry at all, because he's one of those people who rolls with life's ups and downs. He sees the forest for the trees, the mountain from the molehill, or something stupid like that. But I refuse to let the incident slip away and I really don't understand why. I'm not just upset because Andy clocked me with a snowball. The whole aftermath left me with a squeamish feeling, one I spent all weekend trying to shake. Why did Andy have to go and act like a gentleman? He makes me feel small for losing my mind over a mundane practical joke.

Gawd, what a loser he is.

To redirect my emotional upheaval, I decide the time has come to do something spectacular. On the way to lunch, I stop by my locker. Buried under a pile of first term assignments, I find my copy of the student handbook, still in mint condition. I jam the slim book into my purse and head to the cafeteria.

When Jana appears, I glance up from the pages of Harmony High's Rules and Regulations. Apparently someone in district headquarters is also an avid lister.

"It's time for action. We keep talking about doing something, but we haven't achieved anything awesome."

"We're working on it," she says, sliding into the seat next to mine. "We're running. For couch potatoes like us that's super-awesome."

"Yeah, but exercise is *good* for you. I'm talking about

an achievement on the opposite end of the spectrum."

"Like what? You want to start smoking?" She scoots closer and peers over my shoulder. "How about violating the alcoholic beverages policy? We can get drunk before school."

"We'd need a supplier." Mom never brings alcohol home; although she's been known to highly enjoy indulging in adult beverages when out with friends.

"I might be able to sneak a bottle of wine." Jana's parents refer to themselves as oenophiles, meaning they're abnormally fascinated with Pinot Noir and Sauvignon Blanc. They swish and sniff before drinking and stuff like that.

We read on. Jana points to a sternly worded paragraph focusing on underage drinking. "Look here. If we drink alcohol, we'll break a real law, a school rule and possibly serve detention too. Three awesome achievements before first bell." She does a double fist pump in the air.

"Yeah, but if we're caught, we'd be banned from all afterschool activities. We wouldn't be allowed to run track or star in the musical." And we'd definitely get caught. Based on our limited experience draining half-empty wine bottles at Jana's parents' parties, we still have a long way to go before we build up an acceptable booze tolerance.

"Oh, right," Jana says, her mind meeting mine, no

additional explanation needed.

We continue to scan through the seemingly endless number of ways to get kicked out of school.

"Check this out," Jana says, tapping the bottom paragraph of page fifty-three. "There's a zero tolerance policy for obscene language or gestures. Automatic detention."

"I know a few obscene words I'd like to direct at Andy."

Jana looks up from the handbook. "You know, chica, you have an amazing ability to hold onto a grudge."

"It's an exceptional talent that will definitely benefit me later in life."

"If you say so." Jana shrugs. "We could skip homeroom. We only get detention if we're caught."

"Perfect. Tomorrow. We'll hide in the gym."

***

Tuesday morning, Jana stations herself in front of my locker, looking green. She showed up extra early for school just to skip. Hilarious.

"Are you sure about this?" she asks, gnawing away at her bottom lip.

"Relax, Jana, we're not committing a crime. We're skipping homeroom, the most useless twenty minutes of the day."

"Sure, first homeroom and then a full day. Next thing you know, we'll be smoking pot underneath the bleachers."

What a drama queen.

"By the time we work up to marijuana, we'll have graduated. Besides, neither of us can afford a drug habit. We're both broke. All the time."

The first bell rings, sort of a low-decibel fire siren rather than an actual, pleasant, hurry to class please kids, type of sound.

"It's time. We need to hide." Jana's eyes dart up and down the hallway, on the lookout for authority figures.

Just then, a long streak of blue sweatpants, meeting gray sweatshirt, topped with a mess of curly blond hair blurs by. "Morning, ladies. You're late," Andy informs us.

"Thanks, but we're skipping," my best friend says, suddenly developing a backbone.

I cover her mouth with my hand. "Zip it, Jana!"

Too late. Andy's boat-sized feet freeze mid-jog, and his beanpole body bends forward, almost snapping in half. "If you're caught skipping, McCaffrey will throw you out of mathletes," he says, his blue eyes wide behind his thick glasses.

"Oh, the horror!" I say. "No extra calculus."

"Yeah, Andy, you'd better cover for us. The talent drain on the team would be devastating," Jana agrees.

"What's going on here, children?" sounds a male voice behind me. For a second I panic, assuming a teacher has spied us congregating in the hallway and suspects we're up to no good. But the voice is too familiar. I whirl around and catch Dominic Altomeri surveying my backside, which I must say is having one of its better days in my skinny jeans.

"We're skipping, Dom." Jana buffs her nails on her sleeve, appearing totally chill with the class cutting thing. "Want to come with?"

"Excellent. Did I miss something on Snapchat?"

"No," I say. "Jana and I decided to be rebels. Let's hide in the gym."

The three of us turn away from the senior wing. Andy pauses, considering, and then takes off in the opposite direction. "I'll cover for you, but if I'm skipping a class, it's not going to be homeroom. You're already in school and have nothing better to do. At least go to Starbucks or something." He shakes his head in disgust.

"AK is too cool to hang out with the non-genius crowd," Dom says with a low chuckle. The late bell blares, sending the three of us hustling into the gym. We bang open the double doors, and walk right into a teacher's meeting.

Wait. Hold the phone. Does the definition of meeting include tonsil hockey? Hooking up?

Mr. Banks, our WWE Champion-sized gym teacher, has his hands all over Miss Parson, the latest addition to the Harmony High English department. Her skirt is hiked up past the point of decency as she balances on spiky heels, reaching her arms around his pumped up chest.

"Looks like he's showing her the ropes," Dom says.

Jana lets out a startled squeak and then flies back through the open door. Dom hooks his arm in mine and backpedals out of the gym, both of us choking back laughter. He keeps a casual hold on me as we search for Jana. Secretly, I'm thrilled. This is Dominic Altomeri. And he's touching me—Sadie Matthews.

"What now?" Jana asks when we find her crouching behind a glass trophy case, as if that will somehow make her invisible to Principal Dailey. Desperately, I try to devise a new plan while my best friend hyperventilates beside me, shaking in her glitter-covered boots.

This is a perfect example of what happens when you never break the rules. We should have worked our way up to cutting class. Started out by coming in a few minutes late before we jumped right into skipping an entire period.

Before I can formulate a list of alternate hiding spots,

a flash of steel gray hair and black wingtips rounds the corner.

"Dailey!" I hiss.

"Library." Dom spits out the word with the assurance of someone who actually knows how to avoid class-cutting punishment. As total newbies in this department, Jana and I have no choice but to follow him. The three of us high tail it down the steps leading to the freshman hallway. Dom raises a finger to his lips to shush us before tapping open the library door with the finesse of an expert and poking his head inside.

Behind the circulation desk, Mrs. Strong, the librarian, perches on a swivel chair, pecking at her laptop and squawking into the phone. The morning announcements crackle through the old public address system.

Before the door clicks shut behind us, Dom, Jana and I duck behind the closest set of bookshelves. By the time we tiptoe to the far end of the library, our faces are red from holding our collective breaths. Dust flies from the stagnant population of history books, tickling my nose. I struggle to subdue a sneeze as we race to the lounge area and collapse on an overstuffed sofa, still reeling from the shock of the scene we witnessed in the gym, our hands clapped over our mouths to restrain fits of laughter.

"You girls are epic." Dom wraps his arms around us

after we more or less regain control. "I haven't had this much fun since we pantsed Eric Fulman walking out of Spanish last month."

"Ooh. Boxers or briefs?" Jana asks.

"Guess again."

"Boxer briefs?" I venture, hopefully. I picture Eric's massive cheesesteak filled belly, and his pasty white skin. Not exactly a guy I want to see pantsed.

"Nope. None of the above. He was full on commando."

"Yick," Jana says. "Why do guys think pantsing each other is so funny?"

"Humiliation is an important part of high school," Dom says. "Deal with it."

"Has it happened to you?" I ask.

Dom cracks a leering smile. "Wouldn't you like to know?" An obscene image of Dom fills my mind. I shift away from him and fumble with the zipper on my sweatshirt, tugging it all the way up to my neck.

"So, girls, what's next? Are we ditching first period, too?" he asks.

"Not today," I say.

"We wanted to see what we could get away with," Jana says. "You know, test the waters."

"Speaking of water, we should plan a cut day and go to the beach. Swim in the ocean," Dom says.

More images of Dom float through my head. At least this time he's wearing a bathing suit.

"Only if you drive, Dom," Jana coos, batting her long, heavily mascaraed eyelashes at him. She's going to take credit for getting us a ride in his car; I just know it.

Oh, well, I arranged our initial triumph. She would never have skipped homeroom if I hadn't pushed her into it.

I mentally add achievement number one to our list.

Jana and I spend the entire period relaxing on the cushy library sofa, flirting with Dom and planning our next adventure as a threesome.

When the move-to-your-next-class riot alarm wails, Dom leads us between the bookshelves and bends his neck around the corner, checking for Mrs. Strong. Thankfully, she's still fixated on her screen and gabbing away on the phone. As soon as he flashes a thumbs up, the three of us race out of the library.

***

Of course, when I meet up with Andy again in Calculus, I have to deal with his withering look of disapproval. He awaits my arrival, arms folded across his chest, long legs sticking out into the aisle, balancing his workbook on his knee.

"Did you miss me?" I ask, high-stepping over one of his protruding limbs and sliding into my seat. Mrs. McCaffrey scripts a lengthy proof on her SMART board, to the tune of groans from the math haters, who apparently make up a sizable portion of the class.

"Not at all," Andy says, his eyes darting between his workbook and the board. He picks up a pencil and begins to solve step-by-step, his wrist moving rhythmically down the page. His penmanship is so neat that the numbers look digitized. I glance at the trail of formulas and sigh. If he wasn't acting so damn self-righteous, I would beg him for help.

"Homeroom was quiet for once," he continues, circling and underlining his final answer, leaving no doubt about its accuracy. "Mrs. Warren asked if anyone had seen you because you weren't on the call-out list. I told her you felt sick, and Jana walked you to the nurse. You need to stop by the office and ask the secretary to mark you present, or they'll call home looking for you."

"Really? You lied for me? Would that still count as skipping homeroom?" I wonder aloud.

"Do you want it to count?" Andy's light eyebrows pop up above his heavy frames. He probably thought he was doing Jana and me a favor. I scowl up at him, but when our eyes meet the sunlight streaming in the windows seems to bend behind his glasses and illuminate his eyelashes, turning them into wisps of gold. For a second I imagine them turning even lighter in the summer.

"Yes, of course, I want it to count." I snap out of my eyelash fantasy and settle into my work, deciding it's about time to pay attention to Mrs. McCaffrey.

"Why?" he asks, continuing our conversation during the next problem-solving interval.

"Because, Jana and I have this thing going. And skipping homeroom is part of it."

"What's the thing?" He leans forward and rests his elbow on his desk, anxious to hear my answer. Wow, Andy's teetering on the edge of insubordination.

"It's a girl thing. You wouldn't understand."

"Like PMS?"

I burst out laughing. Mr. Smarty-pants is genuinely confused. When Mrs. McCaffrey glances our way, I drop my eyes back to my notebook. "Sure, Andrew, like PMS. Whatever."

We return to class work.

"Hey, what's up with you calling me Andrew?" he asks a few minutes later, after finishing the second problem light years ahead of the rest of us. Over my shoulder, I notice a deep crease develop between his eyebrows, but whether it's due to intense concentration or frustration with my evasiveness, I have no idea.

"Oops. Sorry. My mom uses full names when she's angry, and her habit must have rubbed off on me. I'm still mad about the snowball."

"Oh," Andy says, and I can practically hear the light in his extra–large brain click on. "Actually, I kind of like it. No one calls me Andrew. Besides my mother."

At this revelation, my mouth drops open. I look up from my problem set to find him smiling at me. The corners of his blue eyes crinkle and I think to myself, for the second time, Jana is right. Andy has the potential to move up from a four on the datability meter. The eye crinkling thing gets him to at least a six.

Fill It In – Your Awesome Achievements
To Be Completed By Sadie Matthews and Jana
Rodriguez Prior to June 1st

1. Break a School Rule – Sadie & Jana Cut Homeroom!
2.
3.
4.
5.
6.
7.
8.
9.
10.

Chapter Seven

"How's the daughter of anarchy thing working for you?" Dom asks when I plop down next to him in A.P. Bio.

"So far, so good." I rummage in my backpack for a pen, preparing to copy the lab assignment posted on the blackboard. Animal dissection. Gross.

"Do you vant to drink the blood of pigs? Mwhah Hah Hah."

And today, I'm sitting next to Count Chocula. I shoot him a telling look.

"I need a new partner, then," he says, reverting to his normal tenor. "Someone's gotta do the work while I catch up on my texts."

As he speaks, Dr. Brownstein enters the room, hefting a plastic mail bin. Based on my gut reaction to the odor crawling through the lab, he's definitely not toting paperwork. "Class, we'll need to work in groups of four today. I haven't got enough specimens to go around."

"Want to work with me and Sidh?" Andy leans across the aisle, his blond curls brushing my shoulder. I glance over at Jana's table and notice Arlene is absent.

"Dr. Brownstein, can we work in a group of five?" I ask. "The four of us and Jana?"

"Hoping to avoid being outnumbered by the opposite sex, Sadie?" Dr. Brownstein asks, breaking into a thin-lipped smile. "All right. One group of five. But I expect stellar results from the largest group."

Jana jets over to our lab table and slaps down her notebook. She practically kissed Andy's feet at lunch when she found out how he lied for us in homeroom.

"Thanks again, Andy," she whispers and puckers her lips, sending air kisses in his direction. He smiles down at her. She pats his arm. Since when are Jana and Andy so friendly?

Plunk.

Dr. Brownstein drops a clear plastic bag on the lab table. Inside, our unwitting subject awaits total decimation. The five of us stare at the poor soul, who, once upon a time, was almost a baby pig.

"Gosh, he looks like he's just sleeping," Jana says and sniffs.

"Sidh, read the instructions," Andy says, pushing onward before Jana sinks into hysterics. Sidh clears his throat a few times and holds his notebook in front of his nose. I copy his action, hoping to block some of the eau de swine.

"Fetal Pig Dissection Lab Part One. External Anatomy. Rinse all preservative off the subject."

"Eww. I'm not touching it," Jana says, her voice no longer carrying any trace of sympathy for "the subject."

"Not it. I'll take notes," I say.

Sidh and Dominic both step back from the table; hands raised.

"I'll do it," Andy offers, rolling up his sleeves. He flips on the sink and holds the pig by the hind legs under a stream of running water. The two front legs dangle, and for a second I swear the thing is contemplating a dive down the drain.

"Be careful, Andy," Jana warns. "Don't break him."

"He's already dead," Dom says. "What could be worse than that?"

Sidh reads through a list of features we need to first observe and then describe in excruciating detail. We rely on Andy's familiarity with anatomy as he maneuvers the animal's limbs and points to various body parts. I concentrate on recording our findings. After determining the sex (definitely male), the next step is to slash the poor sucker open.

"Do the honors, AK. You're the only one with medical expertise," Sidh says.

"Are you an EMT?" asks Jana.

"More like a candy striper," Dom interjects.

"His Dad's a doctor," Sidh says and pokes Andy in the arm with a pencil. "Doesn't he take you to work and let you watch him slice and dice?"

"He's a pediatrician," Andy says. "Most of the time he's looking up babies' snotty noses."

"Close enough." Dom nods to Andy. "I vote AK for pig surgeon general."

"You're the best. We owe you lunch or something." Jana shines her mega-watt smile for Andy's benefit.

Andy sucks in a breath and removes a ball of string from the dissection kit. As he ties back the pig's legs, Jana makes a few more sad comments about the poor dead mammal. With the end of the day rapidly approaching, Dom's texts roll in like ocean waves at high tide. He yanks the phone from his pocket and settles back in his chair to tap out replies.

"Scalpel?" Andy asks, doing his finest imitation of a medical professional. Sidh rifles around in the lab kit and comes up with a knife-like instrument, which he hands to Andy, who then opens the pig's stomach in one long cut.

We all lean forward, wrangling for a better view. Even Dom stops texting. The scene turns into something like one of those gross horror movies Jana forces me to watch on our frequently dateless Saturday nights. I'm completely reviled, but unable to look away. The smell of formaldehyde intensifies, and I cover my nose with my sleeve.

"Hey, where's all the blood? Shouldn't it be gushing?" Dom asks. His normally tanned skin pales a bit.

"No, there shouldn't be any blood present. The pig's been drained ahead of time," Andy replies, rooting around in the abdomen with the knife. "Just a bunch of random organs and muscle. I think this is the liver." He stabs a squishy brown body part, plucks it out of the pig's belly and holds it up in front of Dom's nose. Dom goes cross-eyed right before he doubles over and barfs up his lunch.

"Holy Shit!" I scream, gagging and coughing as his stomach contents spurt onto the lab table and my new fuzzy pink sweater. "What the hell, Dominic?"

And that's how I earn my first-ever detention.

Fill It In – February 18th
Ten Ways to Survive Detention

1. Introduce yourself to a group of fellow seniors who call themselves "The Regulars". People you didn't even know existed outside of detention.

2. Count the different hair colors and find one head matching each shade on the rainbow spectrum.

3. Sleep – only if you won't mind that your purse is missing when you wake up.

4. Make a mental list of words rhyming with detention: tension, suspension, comprehension, intervention.

5. Do the wave every time Mr. Banks, this week's featured detention monitor, leaves the room.

6. Answer the question "So, what did you do to get in here?" at least fifty times.

7. Reenact the incident that got you in here with Dominic Altomeri, an "Almost Regular" but not quite a card-carrying member of the detention denizens.

8. Try to earn an early release by holding your breath until you grow faint.

9. Read fifty text messages from Jana apologizing for not cursing as well so we could participate in detention together.

10. Flirt with Dominic. Even though he puked on me. I still want a ride in his car.

Chapter Eight

So, detention is a uniquely terrifying experience. Afterward, I feel the need to go directly home, burn my clothes, and take a long, hot shower. But Jana waits for me, despondent.

"I'm sorry! So sorry!" she gushes.

"What's she upset about? AK should be the one kissing my ass after shoving that organ in my face," Dominic says.

"Andy did apologize," I insist. Profusely. I even thought he was going to cry for a minute or two. And, though he didn't dare say this out loud, I was also under the impression that he was disappointed in the rest of us for ruining his chance at an A in the lab. But once he realized the extent of Dom's puking episode, Andy saved the day by fetching a wad of paper towels from the boys' bathroom and cleaning up the mess. He must not have any form of a gag reflex.

And, in an act of pure cowardice, Dr. Brownstein asked Andy to deliver my punishment.

"How did you not get sick?" I asked when he handed me the pink paper pronouncing my sentence.

"I might not have seen my dad cut people up at work, but after years of spending Saturdays filing paperwork in his office during flu season, I'm pretty immune to vomit," he said, with a touch of pride in his voice.

"Really? I don't think working in your dad's office has had the same effect on my mother." Mom's been a long-time receptionist for Andy's dad's practice. She's strictly front-of-the-house material.

"Your mom can't handle the gross stuff, huh?" He smiled. "Hey, do you need a ride home?"

I stared up at him, amazed, before concluding he was probably trying to be polite. Or he was still attempting to make up for the one-sided snowball fight. Or his guilt over fixing the Senior Superlative vote was eating him up inside.

"No, thanks. I would just stink up your car. The scent of vomit tends to linger."

"Some other time, then."

"Okay, sure," I responded, not really thinking about it. But the lame answer echoed in my mind. Did I just subject myself to a future ride with Andy? Shoot. Maybe he missed my response. I hoped he wouldn't bug me about it every day until I complied.

Anyway, back to Jana's endless string of post-detention apologies.

"Really sorry, Sadie, I mean it," she says, over and over.

"What is it with you two?" Dom asks. "Is it so painful to be apart for an hour? It's like you share a brain or something."

"No, we're best friends," I correct him. "And best friends do not let best friends serve detention alone." I wrap my arm around Jana's shoulders to comfort her. "It was fine though, Jana. I survived. How was track practice?"

"Oh, I, um, kind of skipped. I wasn't in the mood to run alone. Will your detention count for the, you know?" She drops her voice to a whisper. "Or do I still have to go too?"

"I think once is enough for both of us. Fill it in."

Dom lets out a loud huff. "How does anyone talk to the two of you? It's like you have some obnoxious, secret language."

Oops. Forgot about him. "We speak English just like you," I insist.

"Right. So, what are you saying right now?"

"Nothing," Jana says, and "It's a girl thing," I say, at the same time.

"Then shut up. It's been real." He heads for the nearest exit. Before the door slams shut behind him, I spy three cheerleaders perched on the hood of his car. Apparently, Jana and I aren't getting a ride in his Corvette today.

***

Slumped against my locker, recovering from track practice, I hear the fast beat of footsteps approaching. Ben Wexler, senior running star, looks like he's considering performing CPR on my limp, nearly lifeless body.

It didn't take long for me to realize how much I hate running. My legs despise running. My lungs abhor running. Even my brain detests the mind-numbing, repetitive, leg-hammering on the floor action propelling me through the bleak school hallways.

Why am I torturing myself?

Keeping his round, hazel eyes trained on me, Ben glides to a stop. His dark eyebrows stand out like extra-long dashes and they seem to bounce up and down along with the rest of his body as he jogs in place. Although his cheeks are pink from exertion, his breathing appears normal. Meaning he isn't gulping in air like yours truly.

"What do you run? Short or long?" he asks.

A pathetic whimper rises in my burning throat. "Prior to this week, I only ran when I was late for class. Or if my neighbor asked me to walk his dog and I accidentally dropped the leash."

"For real?" Ben rolls his spine forward and touches his toes, all the while staring at me in a disconcerting fashion. He's like an optical illusion, contorting his body in every direction, yet his head never moves. "You decided to try competitive running four months before graduation?"

"I didn't think it would be this hard," I admit. "I guess you've been running for a while?"

"Since third grade." Ben cops a tight smile and glances further down the hall. "What about your friend?"

"Jana? She hasn't run before either."

"Is she seeing anyone?"

Now where did that come from? "Not that I'm aware of."

Ben takes a second to digest my answer. He's known around school as a man of few words. "Keep running," he eventually says. "When you hit a runner's high for the first time – there's nothing like the feeling of all those endorphins kicking through your system."

After imparting this piece of friendly advice, he changes course and sets off in the direction of Jana's locker, leaving me alone to dream about the elusive drug-like effect of running.

***

And guess who actually enjoys running? Jana and both of her left feet. The girl who cannot travel from her locker to homeroom without tripping over some unseen speck of debris in the hallway.

But now, on any given day, Jana beats me to practice by ten minutes and runs warm-up laps with Dominic and Ben while I take my time lacing up my old sneakers.

During the few times the guys separate during practice, like when Dom decides to focus on sprint starts in the gym because the sophomore girls are practicing in there too, I notice Ben hovering near Jana, in an unobtrusive, non-stalkerly way. A casual onlooker might not notice the brief exchange of words passing between the two of them. But, as the most trusted member of Jana's inner circle, I usually hear about these mini-conversations on the way home from practice.

"Wanna run the next circuit with us, Sadie?" Jana

asks. She turns her head, scanning the hallway for me, and almost veers into a row of metal lockers. Without breaking his pace, Ben reaches out his arm and redirects her. Jana's face lights up in a wide smile and she giggles at her misdirection.

Hmmm. Maybe the falling in love achievement she's hoping for isn't as unachievable as I anticipate.

"No more circuits," I plead, sliding bonelessly to the floor. "I need a break." But she's already out of earshot. Every muscle in my body hurts. Gawd. What was I thinking joining the track team?

Fill It In – Your Awesome Achievements
To Be Completed By Sadie Matthews and Jana
Rodriguez Prior to June 1st

1. Break a School Rule – Sadie & Jana Cut Homeroom!
2. **S**erve My First Detention — Sadie
3.
4.
5.
6.
7.
8.
9.
10.

Chapter Nine

After a two grueling weeks of track practice, I crawl four blocks back to my apartment and scale two flights of stairs, feeling my quads pinch with each and every step. I want to crash on the sofa and surf my way through mindless television until I collapse into sleep.

But today is an extra busy day in Sadieland. First, I need to shower because heaven help me I stink worse than the moldy trash bin outside of our building.

Then I need to shovel down some form of sustenance before racing back to school for the spring musical auditions. Combining my less-than-superior culinary capabilities with three cans of black beans, stale bread, and the half jar of peanut butter in our pantry leaves me only limited meal options.

But, as it turns out, I don't need to invent a new dinner recipe. When I enter the apartment, the aroma of homemade spaghetti sauce nearly knocks me back into the hallway.

"What happened to my mother? Did she hit the Powerball jackpot and hire a personal chef?" I sniff the air, cross into the kitchen, and swipe the lid from a simmering pot. A delighted groan escapes my lips at the sight of simmering tomato sauce.

Mom leans against the counter, a look of smug satisfaction on her face. When I smother her with a hug, she bats me away with a claw-shaped utensil.

"Are you kidding me?" I ask. "You're attempting to cook real food?"

"I can cook," she says, a tad bit defensively, running her free hand through her layered brown hair, the same color as mine, but chopped eight inches shorter.

"Theoretically, everyone can cook. I thought you had some strange fear of turning on the oven. Like a traumatic childhood experience related to baked asparagus."

"If that's the case, then I must really be desperate. I thought if I made something you liked, you might take the time to sit down and eat with me." Her eyes meet mine at a level height now that I've caught up to her size-wise. Mom never seems to mind being petite, but I wonder if her attitude would change if I surpassed her in inches.

Even without her direct accusation, I get the idea that it's my fault we've missed each other so much lately. Truth be told, my amped-up activity schedule has cut into the number of hours I spend lounging around the apartment. But Mom is usually pretty busy herself, with her job and her social life (Oldies nights at the bars on Main Street). I've grown accustomed to eating tuna sandwiches solo.

"Do you have plans tonight?" she asks as she scoops pasta out of the pot and hands me a plate. I carry my food to the dining room portion of our cramped apartment, differentiated from the kitchen by a rusty metal strip and a black and white Ikea throw rug under our antique (a.k.a. old and decrepit) table.

"Jana and I are trying out for the spring musical." I settle in and suck my first strand of spaghetti through my teeth. "Auditions start in less than an hour. Aren't you going out, too?"

Tuesday nights are Eighties Dance Jams at The Green Lagoon Pub. My mother's personal form of religion.

"Not until seven."

"Don't you leave early to get a good seat at the bar?"

"I asked Margie to save my regular spot."

"Okay, Mom, but you can't call me before nine, no matter what," I warn her. "This audition is really important." I recite a quick prayer in my head. Please, whoever's up there in heaven looking out for me, grant my mother enough self-control to make it through the night without needing bail money.

"Well, look at you, Miss Actress. I've never seen you so interested in after-school activities. This isn't about a boy, is it?" She appears beside me with a steaming pot and dumps about a billion peas onto my plate. "Because we've talked about letting boys become a distraction."

And then you wind up dropping out of school. Or getting pregnant. I silently add Mom's unspoken worst case scenarios. The ones she's lectured me about for close to eighteen years now. "No boy. Just a last blast of fun before graduation. I'm trying to make the most of my high school years. Maybe learn something new."

"Yes, do that." She sets a water pitcher on the table in front of me. "After high school, life is nothing but a bunch of miserable dead-end jobs and guys with bad breath and ugly shoes hitting on you."

My mother and her wonderfully optimistic view of life.

***

For my first musical audition I throw on jeans and the loose flowery top my grandparents sent me for Christmas, because it's dramatic (or at the very least, eye-catching). After an unanswered, shouted good-bye to Mom, I speed down Main Street to meet Jana. We walk the last few blocks to tryouts belting out Lady Gaga songs to exercise our lungs.

"How bad do we sound?" Jana asks. I catch the fear in her eyes.

"We'll be fine," I say, but I know she recognizes my fear as well.

In the choir room, Leslie fine-tunes her vocal chords with perfectly pitched *Sound of Music* do-re-mi's. Every eight notes, she does some funky type of snorty breathing and sips from a water bottle before restarting back at do-si-do. Jana attempts the same maneuvers, but her tra-la-las sound more like a tone-deaf baby frog.

"I think we're in over our heads," she whispers when the freshmen choirgirls shoot her dirty looks.

"Hey, Sadie-girl! Hey, Jana!" Leslie waves us over when she notices us standing apart from the hard-core drama crowd. "I've already told Ms. Cutler that both of you want to audition for Audrey II. She thinks it's a great idea because the part really calls for more than one person."

"Why would you need two understudies?" I ask.

"Come again?" Leslie frowns, confused. "Oh, no. No, no, no." She cradles her face in her hands and forms an o with her mouth, suddenly comprehending our miscomprehension. "Audrey II isn't an understudy role. Have you not seen the *Little Shop of Horrors* movie?"

She enunciates every word like this is completely unfathomable.

"Uh … no," I reply, as a sweep of terror hits me. The play has the word "horror" in the title. I hate scary stuff. In fact, I pointedly avoid any form of blood and guts, even fake blood and guts. Geez, doesn't everyone in this town already know I barely survived fetal pig dissection?

Just then, Ms. Cutler claps her hands to gain our full attention. Her carroty curls are piled into a messy bun secured with what looks like chopsticks. Heart-shaped purple glasses frame her pale blue eyes, one of which occasionally wanders in the wrong direction.

"Attention, people. And Derek," she says, to the tune of laughter. Jana looks at me helplessly. Missing inside jokes is a bad sign. Breaking through Ms. Cutler's circle of favorites to nab a choice role depends on our ability to scale a mountain of kiss-up, wanna-be Audrey IIs. "Let's begin. Mrs. Bitty, hand out the parts, please."

To set the mood, Ms. Cutler punches a button on the remote in her hand and party music blares from speakers mounted on the wall. Mrs. Bitty, Ms. Cutler's silver-haired assistant and utilitarian piano player, shuffles around the room passing out sample dialogue sketches. She squints at a page titled "Audrey II" and holds it out in front of Jana and me. Together, we shy away.

"Which one of you wants the speaking part?" Mrs. Bitty cackles, revealing a toothless grin.

"Can we both talk?" Jana asks.

"No," Ms. Cutler booms, cutting the music as she speaks. Everyone directs their eyes to Jana and me. "Handling the robotic animation will be enough of a challenge for one person. We need someone to provide a voice-over through an offstage mic."

"I'll do the offstage part," Jana says. "I get stage fright."

"Awesome." Derek Jonas chimes in from across the room. Derek has starred in every school play during our time at Harmony High School. By sheer number of upper-class males present tonight (just him, unless a bunch of senior guys are hiding in the band closet), it looks like he's a shoe-in this time around as well.

"Give Audrey II some Latina flair, Jana," Derek says. "Say the lines real fast, and mix in some Spanish words, like Shakira." He breaks into some sort of flamenco dance and snaps his fingers high above his head.

"Can you sing like Shakira?" Ms. Cutler raises her orangey eyebrows above her purple glasses. "Mrs. Bitty, play a few bars."

"Stop!" Panic consumes Jana's face. "Sorry, Ms. Cutler, but I'm no Shakira."

"But you do a really excellent impression of her," I add, helpfully. Jana's at her screwball best when surfing along on a sugar high. I wonder how many Hershey bars it will take to get her to an Audrey II level of insanity.

"Jana's vocal range won't really matter if she's mic'd offstage," Leslie chirps.

"True," Ms. Cutler agrees. "If you're really that bad, we can always pipe in a recording from the soundtrack."

"And Sadie's size will be an advantage for the onstage part," says Leslie.

"Why, is Audrey II an elf?" I ask. Everyone laughs. I usually ignore the insinuated insults, but by this point in high school, when everyone else has left me far, far behind, vertically speaking, the short jokes get old.

"What?" I ask, searching around for anyone willing to make eye contact and spill the truth. "If she's not short, then what is she?"

"Leafy," says one of the brave sophomore girls on the far side of the room.

"Define leafy." I picture myself dressed as a wood nymph or some other gorgeous mythological creature.

"Audrey II is a plant. A hideous, man-eating plant." Derek scrunches up his ruddy face in what I suppose is mock-horror. "Feed me, Seymour! You know that line, right?"

"I don't know anything. Who's Seymour?"

"The guy who works in the Little Shop of Horrors and loves Audrey the First," Leslie says.

"Wait. Back up a second. Are you saying that not only is my part not a lead role or even an understudy, but it also is not human?"

"Our part," Jana corrects me.

"Your part is a big plant puppet," Derek says.

"But Audrey II *is* a lead role," Leslie insists. "The show can't go on without her. You'll be front and center stage. Isn't that what you wanted?"

"Do Jana and I get top billing on the sign in front of school?"

"Wait, Sadie," Jana raises her hand, as if asking permission to speak. "If we get top billing on the sign, everyone riding by school will associate us with a flesh-eating plant."

"Good point. But, if we take the plant role, will it count for our … thing?"

Jana's head bobs up and down. "Leslie said the show cannot go on without us. Sounds like a fantastic achievement to me."

"Okay, I'm in. But I want to be a sexy plant. With some green sequins or something."

Fill It In – February 20th
Your Lazy Sunday Morning To-Do List

1. Definitely not running.
2. Not attending play practice.
3. Not working on mathlete problems.
4. Not waking up before ten a.m.
5. Not working on college applications.
6. Not cleaning my room. (Sorry, Mom).
7. Not studying for Driver's Ed. (Really sorry, Mom).
8. Not eating breakfast, because there is not one scrap of food to be found in our kitchen.
9. Not waking my mother, because she will hound me about numbers six and seven.
10. I guess I'm going out. Time for an adventure.

Chapter Ten

Although Mom's belly is probably way past full after last night's dinner out with friends, mine sounds like a kitten mewing under my shirt. I hike a half-mile to the grocery store as the purring increases to a full-fledged growl.

Inside Market Fresh, I count out the last of my spending money. I'd done some sporadic babysitting and dog walking for my apartment neighbors, but held off looking for a real job, worried that any commitment to part-time employment will result in the whole awesome achievement list grinding to a dead halt. Jana depends on me to follow through on our mutual promises.

With a sigh, I shove the crumpled bills back into

my wallet. Maybe we can rip through the rest of our achievements in time for me to build my bank account before the money drain of senior week and college. If I ever find a college willing to accept my late application.

Of course, I'm wearing ratty sweats and dirty fake Uggs reserved for sloshing through snow and rain soaked streets. I didn't even bother to fix my ponytail before leaving the apartment, a surefire way to guarantee running into at least one person you don't want to see. So I guess I shouldn't be surprised when I turn into the produce aisle and nearly smack right into Andy and his family.

The Super Ks, as I like to think of them, all spit and polished to perfection. Andy, the oldest child, is shadowed by his middle-school-aged twin brothers, impossible to tell apart, and his younger sister, lagging a few steps behind the bigger boys, chattering nonstop.

Watching the Super K men all shifting their long limbs back and forth awkwardly, obviously out of place in the busy supermarket, I can't prevent a smile from breaking out on my unwashed, oil slick of a face. How Andy gets away with being such a mess is a mystery, because his younger brothers' blond crew cuts remind me of newly shorn sheep. Even the baby sister's shiny blond hair is arranged in tightly braided pigtails.

Hoping to escape notice, I dart behind a tower of crated oranges.

I'm an instant too late.

"Hey, Sadie," Andy calls. I freeze mid-step and glance back to find him looking relieved. Apparently, I'm a welcome diversion to his family outing.

"Uh, hey, Andy."

"Can this be little Sadie Matthews?" I feel Andy's mom looking me up and down.

I paste a smile on my face and turn to greet her. "Hi, Mrs. Kosolowski."

She pats the side of her blond hair, pulled into a tight bun and sprayed to the consistency of a stone monument. I pry my fingers from the handle of my shopping basket and shake her hand. It feels like the polite thing to do.

"Your mother showed me your graduation picture when I stopped in the office last week," Mrs. Kosolowski says. "I told her you've grown into a beautiful young woman. Gorgeous."

Heat creeps into my face. Gorgeous is not an adjective anyone uses to describe me. Jana is the gorgeous one. I'm her cute but boring sidekick. Too embarrassed to meet Andy's gaze, I pick up a Granny Smith apple and toss it into my basket. He must also be mortified by the way his mother's fawning over me. I hope she doesn't know about our attempted arranged marriage, courtesy of the senior class.

"Sweetheart, have you eaten breakfast?" she continues.

"No, actually, I haven't," I admit, and then experience the awful realization that this was not the answer I should have provided.

"Then, please, stop by our house on your way home."

"Mom makes waffles on Sundays if we don't get thrown out of church," one of the little short-haired Andy clones says, his voice dripping with fake excitement. The other twin rolls his eyes at the blatant bribery.

"Has that happened?" I ask, amazed.

"Only once. But Andy saw the dead mouse first. He told me to pick it up, so you wanna guess who got in trouble when Mrs. Dalton fainted?" twin one says.

"I said get rid of it. Instead, you dangled a dead rodent in the ninety-year-old woman's face," Andy says.

"Andrew never gets blamed for anything," says twin two.

Twin one snorts. "Yeah, Mom won't turn her head to look at him because she's afraid Monsignor would catch her not paying attention."

In the midst of their family squabble, my stomach sends a loud and clear message, deciding to accept the breakfast invitation without consulting my brain.

"Um …" I look to Andy for help. He grins, knowing full well how easily food entices me.

"Mom's waffles are the best in town," he says, with a touch of pride.

"Oh. Well. If you don't mind an extra person." I've never eaten an actual homemade waffle. My mother and I are Eggo connoisseurs.

"The more, the merrier," Dr. Kosolowski says. Behind his bifocals, his blue eyes crinkle when he grins, exactly like Andy's. I convince myself I'm suffering the effects of low blood sugar.

"I'm not really dressed," I say, still hesitating.

"Don't worry, Thadie. I'm ditching this dreth as thoon as I get home," little Andyette chirps, her voice whistling through the gap in her mouth where two front teeth are missing. Everyone laughs.

"Okay, then. Uh, sure. I'll come. Who can resist waffles?"

"I'll help Sadie check out and walk her to our house." Andy steps away from his family. "In case she doesn't remember where we live."

"Of course I remember," I say. As if I could ever forget. His house is only a few blocks from downtown Harmony, across the invisible line separating those of us with tiny living spaces from those with huge Victorian-style estates situated on acres of wooded property. Kosolowski Manor is practically a landmark. Actually, I think it was recently designated a historical structure. I bet George Washington slept in Andy's bedroom or something like that.

"So, do you always go food shopping together?" I ask, as he lopes along beside me on the way to the dairy aisle. My question must startle him out of some ultra-intelligent daydream because he takes a minute to answer.

"Oh, um, not really. Mom wanted to stop at the market since it's on our way home from church."

"Wow. I can see who wears the pants in your family."

Andy grins. "She's the boss."

Apparently fearing I may bail on breakfast, he stands guard while I buy time carefully selecting a gallon of milk. I reach all the way in the back of the dairy case for the one with the furthest expiration date, allowing cool air to brush over my warm cheeks.

By this point, I'm having difficulty remembering why I even left my apartment.

I heft a gallon from the back row, trying not to bend forward too much when I feel my sweatshirt riding up my back. As soon as I drop the milk into my plastic basket, Andy reaches out to take it from me.

"I've got it," I protest, swaying back and forth while we play tug-of-war.

"It's no problem." He stands firm until I release my grip on the handle. Maneuvering the basket higher on his arm, he heads toward the checkout counter. Halfway down the aisle, he reaches his free hand around to tuck in his shirt, revealing his ribbed corduroys stretched tightly over his posterior. My eyes immediately fuse on his retreating form. It strikes me how conditioned I am to seeing Andy in grungy sweats at school. Is that why I never bother to really look at him this way?

After a couple deep, steadying breaths, I emerge from a disoriented haze and remind myself Andy is still Andy, no matter if he's dressed in sweats or nice pants. Before I'm led further astray by his argyle socks, I chase him to the checkout, cutting him off so he doesn't pay for my groceries.

Chapter Eleven

Traffic sails by as Andy and I stroll through town. I take two steps for every one of his long strides, but at least he keeps the pace slow. As we walk, I tell him about the *Little Shop of Horrors* audition, and how I ended up taking on the role of a carnivorous plant.

Keep the conversation light and friendly, I remind myself over and over. Just so I can surreptitiously observe Andy's eye-crinkling and make sure that it's not as cute as I imagined. Plus, Andy's evil, axe-murderer/Muppet laugh should cure my current bout of irrationality. Seriously, the words cute and Andy cannot possibly belong in the same sentence.

But hunger-induced lightheadedness must cloud my

senses. When Andy laughs at my description of Audrey II, his "heh-heh" sets off a flash of joy inside of me. Andy's laughter has somehow morphed into a positive attribute. And combined with his blue eyes, sparkling like sea glass behind his heavy frames, he looks, I don't know, on the verge of appealing?

"So is your interest in drama the reason you haven't been at mathletes?" he interrupts my no-holds-barred attempt at small talk.

"Not at all. Play practices are at night. After school, Jana and I are running track. Wait, you noticed we were missing?"

"Did you think you could skip mathletes without anyone noticing?" He fakes a look of amazement.

I smile. "It's not like Jana and I are an integral part of the team. We just like to talk to Mrs. McCaffrey about girl stuff."

"You also provide mathletic entertainment. Practicing routine functions isn't as much fun without the Jana and Sadie dynamic duo." His voice carries a trace of wistfulness. "I like how you always do a ten-second countdown when I'm working on lightning round problems."

I scoff. "Anyone in mathletes can count backward from ten to one. If not, the team is in trouble."

"Heh-heh. And you're the only person who cheers when I get the whole worksheet correct. But, you're probably making fun of me, right?"

"Um, not one hundred percent making fun. Deep down, I'm extremely impressed. I've never aced a worksheet the way you do," I confess, craning my neck skyward to catch his expression. He's not looking at me, though, just swinging his head back and forth to check out the leftover Valentine's Day decorations hanging in the shop windows.

Ugh. Big pink hearts and a red foil cupid aiming an arrow directly at Andy's mess of blond curls. I must be delusional. For some reason, I imagine Melinda Banner popping out from behind a pine tree, camera in hand, looking for the truth behind the Senior Superlatives. I step to the side, adding space between Andy and me.

"Here, let me carry the groceries." I reach for the bag.

He moves it to his other hand, out of my reach. "We invited you, so I'll carry this. You didn't plan on walking all over town with a gallon of milk."

He casts his bright, blue eyes my way again and without warning, I plunge into freak out territory. I can't stop looking at him, and he's openly staring back.

Geez, I need to stop overthinking this Andy stuff. Andy is supposed to be Andy. You know, a geeky guy who knows everything about everything. Annoying, right? Not in any remote way physically attractive. Andy should not be permitted to pay me compliments and carry my bags through town.

But I'm not fighting very hard to get my stuff back, am I?

Hung up on this question, I stumble on a crack in the uneven pavement. Andy reaches out a hand to steady me before my knees scrape concrete.

"Shoot. Thanks."

"No problem." Once I'm balanced, he removes his hand from my arm and launches into a warbling, off-key tune about lots of beer, a pickup truck, and a broken heart.

"Country? Really? I pegged you as more of a smooth jazz kind of guy."

In answer, he increases his obnoxious caterwauling. Squirrels scratch their claws over bald tree limbs to drown out his horrific tonality. When Andy repeats the refrain a third time, I surrender and join in, laughing my way through the chorus. Deciphering country music lyrics isn't rocket science, unlike most of Andy's preferred verbal interactions.

Together, we must wake up half of Harmony before arriving at the end of his driveway. At least the musical interlude distracts me from my discomfort over the Sunday morning version of Andy. That's a road I can't let myself follow. Ever.

We step inside the Kosolowski's mud room. Andy kicks off his shoes and a wave of panic crushes me. Under my fake Uggs, my socks are filled with toe and heel holes. And I'm pretty sure those same socks have been worn at least two days in a row, because their prior location was my bedroom carpet.

Quickly, I decided politeness trumps embarrassment, so while Andy hangs my jacket on a wall hook, I tear off my socks and stuff them inside of my boots.

"What color is that?" Andy points to my painted toenails.

I feel like my entire body is naked, not just my feet. "Um, I think it's called Purple Passion."

"Cool." And with that un-Andylike comment, he ducks out of the mudroom, into the large open kitchen where the rest of his family preps breakfast in assembly line fashion, standing around a huge granite-topped island. Breakfast scents of cinnamon, coffee, and maple syrup swirl in the warm air. The room goes a little fuzzy, and I cut off a delighted gasp before embarrassing myself.

Andy opens the refrigerator and pours himself a glass of water, his eyes glued to a football game playing on the television.

"Andrew, did you get Sadie a drink?" Mrs. K. asks the instant before the glass touches his lips. Somehow she caught him without even glancing up from the bowl of egg whites she's whipping with a small appliance resembling a mini-torture device. Andy passes me the glass and reaches back in the fridge for the water pitcher.

At Mrs. K.'s request, the younger Kosolowskis set the long plank table in the center of the kitchen. When their mother turns her back, the twins toss plates from the cabinet to the table while Andy's sister counts aloud the number of forks she picked from the drawer. Geez. This family is so un-dysfunctional that they're abnormal. I take a step backward, separating myself from their closeness, and watch Mrs. Kosolowski fold the egg whites into the batter with a huge paddle, another instrument that could double as a parental weapon against misbehaving children.

Then Dr. Kosolowski tosses his tie over his shoulder, pulls out a cast iron skillet and begins frying bacon. I suppress a smile. The physician who lectures my mother on the benefits of force-feeding broccoli to youngsters is flipping grease-soaked meat with heavy, metal tongs.

"Sadie, have you ever used a waffle machine?" Mrs. Kosolowski notices me standing against the wall. "Andrew tends to over-pour, which spills the batter. But I bet you'll have a knack for this." She demonstrates the correct technique before handing me the ladle. I drizzle batter in the center of the grid, close the machine and quickly flick my wrist. The machine completes its one-eighty before anything oozes out. Everyone applauds my success.

Actually, the Kosolowski family does a lot of cheering

and clapping. They celebrate every one of life's little victories.

As I manufacture a steady stream of waffles, hoping to appease the twins' nearly insatiable appetites, Andy stands at the sink behind me, washing strawberries and slicing bananas. Andy's sister sets up a buffet of toppings in glass bowls. Mini chocolate chips, granola and rainbow sprinkles.

"This isn't breakfast, it's dessert," I say, and Andy throws me a quick grin over his shoulder. When I finally manage to outpace the demand, I lower myself into a seat at the table and dig in. For the next hour, I indulge in enough calories to cover my three meals for the day and then some. The Super Ks are nonstop talkers; their conversation peppered with good-natured taunts and private jokes, some of which the twins take the time to explain to me.

Eventually, though, I remember my mother, waking up alone in our sad little apartment.

"Thanks so much, Mrs. K., but I have to go." I pop one last syrup coated strawberry in my mouth before placing my empty plate by the sink.

"It was nice seeing you again, Sadie," Mrs. K. says. "Tell your mother she has every right to brag about you."

My insides cringe. Mom has been known to stop random people on the street and mention that her daughter recently made the honor roll. I can't imagine what she says to her unfortunate captive audience of coworkers and their spouses stopping by the office.

"Andrew, walk Sadie out," Mrs. K. says. Andy drops his silverware and rises from his seat.

I wave him back down. "I'm fine. I'll see you tomorrow."

"Andrew." Mrs. Kosolowski directs a stern mom-look toward her son. He gets the message. So do I.

Andy removes my groceries from the refrigerator, which I completely forgot about in my current food-induced walking coma. He waits for me to slip on my boots. We walk to the end of the driveway in silence. I sense that he wants me to say something, so I give it a shot.

"Thanks, Andy. I would return the favor, but I don't have a waffle maker at my disposal."

"You could take me out for breakfast," he says, his eyes perking up and doing the happy twinkling thing again. "Or I could take you."

"Maybe I'm being dense, but how does you taking me out equal me returning a favor to your mother for inviting me to breakfast?"

"You're right. It's stupid." The words rush from his mouth. He hands me the plastic bag then shoves his hands in his pockets. "Just send my mom a thank you note. She eats that stuff up."

And without even a see you later, he disappears inside of his house.

Fill It In - Random List
Sadie's List of Reasons to Move in with the Kosolowskis

1. Increased closet size would allow me to stash a greater inventory of clearance rack items.

2. Their pantry shelves are fully stocked. No one would notice how much covert snacking takes place.

3. I bet Mrs. K. could use help with the little Super Ks because Andy is busy studying. I could live with them and earn money too.

4. Ditto for waffle making and other cooking and household chores.

5. I hate how everyone thinks that because I'm an only child there's something wrong with me. Like I had anything whatsoever to do with my lack of siblings. It's not as if I was such a freak that my dad moved away even before I was born, vowing never to return, and my mom refused to consider having another child after raising me. Okay, I'll admit, I don't know that for sure.

6. Thanks to Mrs. K.'s secret recipe, I now dream about waffles. Camping out in her kitchen is the best way to feed my addiction.

7. If I told Mrs. K. I was playing the part of a big green plant in the school musical, I'm sure she wouldn't fall out of her chair from laughing so hard like my mom did.

8. The Kosolowskis must have a maid because no way can four kids live in a house as spotless as theirs is. So unless they want to pay me to work (see numbers 3 and 4), no need to worry about cleaning my room.

9. They have TVs strategically placed around the house so you can watch your shows no matter where you're sitting at the kitchen table. In my apartment that's physically impossible unless I sit on the floor with my plate on my knees. Even then, my neck hurts when I look up.

10. I would be part of a big family. I love my mom, but sometimes I wish I knew what that feels like—both the joy and the pain.

Chapter Twelve

"You never called me back yesterday." Jana pounces the minute I open my locker, ready for a pre-homeroom gossip fest.

"I accidentally left my bedroom door open." One clue as to how much breakfast with Andy's family threw me off. Based on my afternoon-long stupor, I wouldn't have been surprised if someone told me Mrs. K. mixed a few questionable spices in her waffle batter. "My mom freaked out, and I spent the day cleaning up the mess."

No way can I mention breakfast with Andy's family. Jana would question me to death about a nonevent.

"Ooh, did you find my silver sandals? The ones you borrowed last summer? Under your bed or something?"

"Still no sign of your fancy footwear. Colette must have taken them, not me."

"I remember you asking for them. Besides, Colette can't squeeze her mammoth toes in those shoes." Jana lifts her foot to model a black sequined-covered boot. "Do you like these? Are they too middle school?"

"On me, they would look middle schoolish. But they work for you."

She points her toe and the sequins ripple under the yellow florescent lights. "Darn right they do."

"What happens when you step in a puddle?"

Jana shrugs, unconcerned. "I ran across the street to make the green light on the way to school and lost about thirty sequins."

"I guess you're not expecting to take them with you to college, then."

As we work our way down the senior hallway, I notice Andy stacking his books into a neat pile on the top shelf of his locker. Despite his just-got-trampled-on appearance, he's the king of organization when it comes to schoolwork.

"Yoo-hoo! Hi, Andy!" Jana calls. I develop a sudden fascination in the SAT Prep Course flyer hanging on the opposite side of the hallway.

"Morning, Jana," Andy answers in a somber tone. "Sadie." I glance over when I hear my name. He nods in my direction.

"Wow, who died?" Jana asks, a little too loudly, as I stand there wishing she would be the one to keel over. Not literally, of course. But sometimes Jana opens her mouth and inserts her foot. Repeatedly.

I wonder if Andy's still fuming over our breakfast payback conversation. Did I say something completely offensive? I was genuinely confused, and he didn't seem to want to bother clearing things up. I rewind the discussion in my head. After my inane response, he must have realized I could never match his level of brainpower, and simply grew tired of dumbing down our verbal sparring.

Irritated by his attitude, I hurry forward, adding space between us. Jana rushes to catch up, ready to continue her footwear discussion.

***

In Calculus, Andy lives on, enraptured by the latest set of equations posted on the SMART board. He barely glances up when I pass him on the way to my desk. Before diving into math, I tear off the corner of a page in my notebook and scribble a short note.

Thanks again for the waffles. Are we OK?

I toss the slip of paper over my shoulder.

Mr. Perfect Student behind me isn't about to miss our favorite teacher's lecture on the squeeze theorem, so his reply doesn't come until Mrs. McCaffrey assigns independent work. He slides a paper under my arm, onto my desk.

We're ok. Nothing's changed.

Well, duh. How could a little thing like breakfast with the Kosolowskis alter my entire outlook on life? The tight sensation in my chest evaporates. No messy situation to deal with on the Andy front.

***

By the time A.P. Bio class rolls around, I'm ready to move on, hoping my secret waffle interlude with Andy has died a quiet death. But when Dom asks in a totally uninterested manner about my weekend, my heart freezes for a second and then reignites with one loud thump. In my peripheral line of vision, I notice Andy's head tilt sideways.

"Same old," I say.

"What about you, AK?" Dom asks. "What'd you do? Star Wars Convention?"

I grip the side of the lab table, bracing for Andy's answer.

"Nope. Just the usual."

I need to stop worrying about Andy telling everyone we spent the morning together. Obviously, it meant nothing to him. Right now, his biggest concern seems to be decoding Sidh's handwritten list of homework assignments, ones Andy missed because he took a day off from school last week to check out MIT for the millionth time. Probably on the VIP tour.

"Lame," Dom says, slumping back in his chair and yawning. "Sadie, can I see your notes? Cause I need to make sure I've got everything down before the test tomorrow."

He reaches for my three ring binder with all my class outlines printed out, arranged by subject, and highlighted appropriately. Without bothering to wait for my reply, he flips it open and begins taking pictures with his cell phone.

"I need to know what you think is important," he explains. "Limits my study time."

For the next forty-three minutes, Andy ignores me, his body as stiff as an extra-long surf board, or perhaps a half-dead person settling into the early stages of rigor mortis. This tempo of silence continues the next day as well. I thought he would at least bring up the fact that

I downed four waffles just to get a rise from me. But he doesn't speak to me or about me at all.

In fact, Andy Kosolowski has the nerve to totally ignore me for the rest of the week.

Of course, I'm beyond happy about it. Relieved, more like it. I've got so much else going on, with track, my role as a musical plant, coming up with more crazy achievements before graduation, and schoolwork. Who wants to deal with a temperamental genius?

***

After school, I run into Melinda Banner in the girls' locker room, looking neat and perfect in her basketball uniform. She tugs her auburn hair into a severe ponytail, with not one strand escaping.

"Oh, Sadie, I've been meaning to ask you something about the Senior Superlatives," she says, opening a top-row locker, blocking my view of her face.

I prop my left foot on a bench and pull my laces tighter. "Sure. Whatever."

"It's just that I interviewed Cindy and I talked to Andy for my last article, but not you."

"I guess I'm pretty forgettable." Sarcasm drips from

my voice.

She closes the locker door and shifts her gaze to me. We stare at each other for a long minute. "So. What happened?"

The hair on the back of my neck prickles. "I have no idea."

She raises an eyebrow. "Andy and Cindy both claimed they had nothing to do with the results. And no one I've spoken with off-the-record admits to voting for you. So..."

"So what? You think I fixed it?" I'm aware of the screech in my voice.

"I don't know. Did you?" she asks, a hint of a smile playing on her lips.

"No. Never. Not at all. And you can quote me on that."

Her smile widens. "Thanks. Maybe I will." As she saunters away, I feel sick all over again.

Reeling after the showdown with Melinda, I dog it in practice, running miles behind the rest of the girls. Even Jana laps me three times. She slows to my pace during our last circuit of the day, chatting away the whole time about homework, our weekend plans, and our unachieved list items. Strangely, the person incapable of walking a straight line excels at simultaneously running *and* talking.

"Everything okay?" she asks.

I force hot air out of my lungs with a long, slow breath. "Miranda Banner's nosing around about the Senior Superlatives."

"About that, or about Andy?"

I shrug. "She's a pain in the ass."

"Everyone else in school has forgotten about it. Does the whole thing with Andy still bother you?"

"No, but she bothers me."

"Must be a slow news day at Harmony. No one's Instagrammed an ugly picture of themselves by accident." We turn down the junior hallway. "Ben mentioned he and Dominic may drive to Philly this weekend for the car show. Do you think it would look obvious if we took the train into the city and happened to run into them?"

I see her mouth moving and hear her voice ringing in the air around me, but my oxygen deprived brain needs fifty more meters to process her suggestion.

"Since we don't drive and have zero interest in cars, yes," I answer as we curve around the trash can Coach Jenkins placed in the junior hallway to indicate when we're permitted to change direction.

"I was thinking it might somehow count as an achievement," Jana says, somewhat unconvincingly.

"That's the only reason?"

"Sure."

She's holding out, big time. "Is it Dominic?"

"No."

Then it's Ben.

"Ben's cute," I wheeze, from the bottom of my aching chest.

"He's alright," she answers with a noncommittal wave of her hand. Her voice trills, indicating otherwise. Quiet Ben gains a spot on the Jana Rodriguez potential boyfriend scale.

"Did you finish your English paper?" she asks after we round the next corner.

The sore muscles in my neck throb harder when I turn to look at her. "Really? You want to talk about homework?"

"What else are we supposed to do?" she asks, twirling her pony tail around her finger as she ambles along in a slow jog.

"Run," I pant.

"I can't just run. It's soooo boring."

"More like excruciating. Why are we doing this?"

"Because, chica, we don't give up!"

"Even though signing up for track might be the stupidest idea we've ever had?"

"No, it's not stupid. We're not coasting through life anymore. We found a purpose. Set some goals."

"Right now, my only goal is to remain upright."

***

If Coach Jenkins is like an Army General running boot camp worthy track practices, then Ms. Cutler wins the title Queen of Spazland. When we practice *Little Shop of Horrors*, she jumps from scene to scene, her orangey curls flying in every direction at once. By the end of the night, she's the one looking like she just ran a marathon. Coach Jenkins barely breaks a sweat, even after two hours of nonstop barking about improper form.

Play practice typically kicks off with Mrs. Bitty on the piano, leading vocal warm-ups. Next, we sing each of the songs as a group.

By the end of these sing-a-longs, I'm usually praying for an escape. The words stick in my head, replaying over and over like worms squiggling through my brain. Ugh.

Since the robotics club has yet to unveil what they promised to be a sexy plant apparatus, (X-rated is not permitted, according to Ms. Cutler, but a limited amount of "sensuousness" is okay), I devote most of my mandatory rehearsal time to hanging backstage with Jana and the stage crew, listening to Leslie and Derek run through various scenes. Derek struggles with memorization, and he repeatedly flubs lines, to everyone's snickering enjoyment. Everyone, except Ms. Cutler, that is.

"You need to spend some quality time with the script, Derek. Come see me during study hall," she says. "Mrs. Bitty, take that song again from the top." Mrs. Bitty's spine curves over the piano, her nose brushing the sheet music as she squints at the notes. Although her arthritic fingers skip over a good portion of the melody, no one bothers to bring this to her attention. Leslie says when we're mic'd up during the show no one will hear the accompaniment anyway.

"Thank goodness I don't have to memorize my lines. I keep a copy of the script offstage," Jana whispers.

"And thank goodness I just have to stand there and act like a plant," I say.

"A horrific, man-eating plant."

"A horrific, man-eating plant bearing a strong resemblance to a glittery head of kale with a diva complex," I add and we break into laughter. The stage crew guys throw angry glares our way, not wanting to be blamed for our misbehavior.

"Tell me again, Sadie. Why are we doing this?" Jana asks, once we regain our ability to speak.

"Because we can't graduate to real life without subjecting ourselves to this wonderfully awesome experience!" We do our own version of a fist bump combined with a secret handshake, a series of synchronized hand and finger movements we've worked on since kindergarten.

Chapter Thirteen

Mr. Drum administers his final Driver's Ed exam on the last Saturday of February. If I pass, Mom promises to let me retake my permit test. After that, I just need to find someone brave enough to spend sixty-five hours in the passenger seat while I practice driving.

The night before the final, I sleep over at Jana's house, assuming we'll spend a few hours cramming. What we actually do is flop on her bed in front of a zombie love story, (still scary, though billed as a chick flick) with all of the bedroom lights on and the closet doors open.

Between scenes, we pause the DVD and quiz each other on driving laws.

"Friday night studying goes against our principles,"

Jana complains.

"I'm all for violation in this case. I can't deal with one more Saturday morning stuck in class listening to sophomores bragging about the new cars they got for their sixteenth birthdays."

Jana frowns. "You're right. At this rate, Colette will be driving before me. She's already pushing my parents for a car. Baby girl gets everything in this house."

I'm tempted to remind Jana that her sister shares a bathroom with their younger brother. Totally gross, in my opinion. I'd definitely ask for a car as payback.

"Let's study." I crack open our Driver's Ed manual. "What is the minimum distance allowed between a parked vehicle and a stop sign?"

"Fifteen feet? No, that's a fire hydrant. Thirty. It's thirty!" Jana shovels a handful of popcorn in her mouth.

"Ding ding ding! Correct!"

Jana jumps off the bed and slaps the wall, right where her posters of The Vamps and Shawn Mendes used to hang. "We've got this! I can't wait to sleep in on Saturday mornings."

***

The next morning, after Jana and I deflate a stack of pancakes, Mr. Rodriguez offers to drive us to class. He's not much taller than Jana, a well-trimmed man with jet black hair. Even though he focuses on immigration law at his small firm, on special occasions such as this frosty winter morning, he insists on interrogating his daughter about driving regulations.

"Tell me how long your license will be revoked if you're caught driving under the influence," he says as we motor along the side streets of town.

Jana slumps against the side door. "If your last name is Rodriguez? Forever."

"Longer than a forever," he says.

"Enough, Father. Mr. Drum showed us tons of pictures of DUI crashes. Besides, he's mainly worried about our driving skills when we're sober."

"Texting, then," Mr. Rodriguez continues in his clipped voice, which still carries a trace of his Cuban heritage. "You kids are transfixed by those screens. Tell me, petunia, what is the penalty for texting while driving?"

"Really bad. I won't do it. Ever."

"Yes, because aside from the legal ramifications, you do realize the parental punishment would be significantly worse, am I right?"

"Yes, Father," Jana answers, with an annoyed sigh.

"That's my girl. Go get 'em, daffodil." Mr. Rodriguez lives to embarrass Jana with his flowery nicknames. He's been at it for years, and always feigns innocence when she brings the awful habit to his attention. I consider Jana's mortification as one more reason I'm happy my dad lives on the opposite side of the country—one less person to humiliate me in public.

We follow our fellow non-driving classmates into school. The completion of Driver's Ed creates a class-wide buzz large enough to rival the effects of a dozen super-sized mocha macchiatos.

"Open your test booklet and begin immediately." Mr. Drum waves us into the room, as if he, too, is excited to free up our seats in his class.

I speed through thirty multiple-choice questions, circling the correct answers on defensive driving, proper seat belt use, and most efficient steering techniques. Next, I crank out a bunch of true and false answers. Excitement rises in my chest. I know this stuff! Somehow, while I vegged out in class the last six Saturday mornings, the driving code sank into my head.

I zoom through two pages of diagrammed intersections, scrawling arrows to indicate the right of way and correct traffic patterns. (Not necessarily the biggest car first, as I now know).

I turn to the final section. A list! I am so acing this exam.

Give five examples of driving distractions and explain how to avoid them.

My responses:

1. Cell phones – turn them off.

2. Loud music – keep it down.

3. Food – resist the call of the McDonald's drive thru.

4. Putting on makeup – you don't need to look good when driving.

5. Mr. Drum – because he's so hot I forgot how to drive.

"Jana," I whisper. At the sound of her name, she rips her eyes from her test, looking frazzled. She must not be doing as well as me. I slide my list to the edge of my desk for her to read before I erase and revise my answers. But Mr. Drum notices my answer-sharing and reaches my seat in three, lightning-fast strides.

"Finished, Miss Matthews?" He yanks the booklet out of my hand. His arm sweeps in front of my face, granting me an eye-level view of his forearm tattoos, an inked assortment of lethal weapons. Like a curved ninja sword. And I think something called a sickle decorates his elbow.

I shrink back into my seat. "Um, not quite. Can I please have my test back, Mr. Drum?"

"No. You're done now. Everyone else, five minutes. Final grades will be posted next week." Without bothering to wait for Mr. Drum to discover exactly why I will fail Driver's Ed, I grab my backpack and run.

Fill It In – February 27th
Top Ten Ways To Screw Up Your Life

1. Write that your teacher is hot on your test paper.

2. Decide to show said paper to your best friend who is completely clueless.

3. Get voted "Most Likely to Marry" someone in your class when you are not even dating that someone. Or have ever thought about that person in that way.

4. Try to come up with 10 totally impossible achievements to complete by the end of the school year when really you should be applying to colleges and writing your American Government term paper.

5. Agree to wear a leafy, green-sequined costume for the school musical.

6. Join the track team.

7. Notice boys with glasses who have bright blue eyes that sparkle when they smile.

8. Cut your hair into a chin length bob because you don't feel like washing it every day. It takes years to grow out. I mean, years! Almost there, though.

9. Fantasize about your lab partner when you're supposed to be taking notes, because he sure isn't.

10. Fall in love with the wrong person.

Chapter Fourteen

I did not just write Mr. Drum is hot on my test paper.

Yes, I did.

Seriously. It's like I carry a big bag of stupid around with me and continually pull stuff out of it.

As I cross back through town, putting as much distance as possible between me and the Driver's Ed classroom, a sharp whistle knocks me out of my fog. Sidh calls my name from the opposite side of the road, where he's walking with Andy. Discretely, I check for leftover patches of snow nearby.

When the light changes, they cross over to my side of the street.

"Don't you two have anything better to do besides

hang out in front of the bakery?"

"Not really," Sidh says, shrugging off my question. "We were playing hoops at the open gym. AK and I rule the loser league."

"What's the looser league?" I ask, unable to make the connection between being loose and playing basketball.

"No. Loooo-ser," Sidh drawls.

"The intramural league for those of us who can't compete at the high school level," Andy says, cluing me in on the real deal.

"Dude, we couldn't compete at the third-grade level," Sidh says. Andy smiles his good-natured smile, in total agreement.

"Ha-ha. I'm sure you guys rule the loooo-ser league. Since I'm here, does one of you want to throw something at my face?" I spread my arms, offering a wide target.

"Are you going to ride me about that until I die, Sadie?" Andy snaps. Wow. Angry Andy is a new experience for me. I wonder if his head is going to split in two and send his blond curls flying all over Main Street.

"Uh, no. Sorry. I'm done now. See you around." I hike my backpack over my shoulder and continue on.

A couple blocks later, I hear two large sneakers thwacking the concrete sidewalk behind me. Before I can duck into the side alley, Andy calls my name.

"Yes, Andy?" I swing around and clutch it in front of

me, an instinctive defense mechanism.

"I want to know something. What's with your attitude? Was the snowball such a big freaking deal?" Patches of deep red appear on his cheeks.

"No. It wasn't," I admit.

"I thought we were friends again after the éclairs. And breakfast at my house."

I swallow hard, feeling like a terrible person. "I thought so too. But you stopped talking to me."

"You ignored me first," he shoots back, sounding like a sixth-grader.

"Not on purpose," I lie. "Maybe we misunderstood each other. And right now, you're catching me after a really bad Driver's Ed class."

"What happened?" Half of Andy's mouth twitches into a smile. "Did you back up over your teacher?"

"Gawd, no. I'm not even up to the driving part yet. And I never will be at the rate I'm going."

"You haven't passed the permit test? It's the same ten questions every time; they just mix up the order. At least, that's what I heard. I only took it once."

"Of course you did. But I can't even get to that point if I keep messing up the stupid class. I must have some type of mental block." A mental block shaped like a former Army Ranger turned motorcycle dude who happens to be my instructor.

Andy looks ready to spit out some snarky retort, but wisely holds back. "I can help you," he says instead.

"How so? Can you teach me to drive?"

"Sure. Or fly, even. I've been taking lessons at the Harmony airport. I have airtime scheduled this afternoon."

"You're piloting an airplane, and I'm still walking to school?" I shake my head. "I am such a total loser."

"You're not a loser. I'm just —,"

"An exceptional overachiever?"

"Something like that." Behind his glasses, Andy's blue eyes do that magical twinkling thing. He shoves his hands in his pockets and continues. "As soon as I was old enough for flying lessons, I begged my parents to sign the paperwork. They watched me build model airplanes and rockets for years."

"Airplane-building is more Andy-style. Flying heavy machinery, not so much. I pegged you as a two feet on the ground kind of guy."

"Yeah, but I need to know how to operate what I design. And, statistically, flying is completely safe. It's just a bunch of math and physics."

I nod in fake agreement. "Right. You would know."

"Plus, I haven't soloed yet. My instructor copilots until I pass the written exam. And I can't take that until this summer."

As he talks, he looks down at me, and I look up at

him. Our eyes meet somewhere in the middle and we both pause as something uncomfortable passes between us. A bird chirps on a branch nearby, sounding loud enough to shake the earth. I spy a green bench ahead of me and head over to take a seat, breaking our connection.

Andy watches me toy with the strap on my backpack. He shifts his weight from one leg to the other, considering. Eventually he joins me on the bench, stretches his long legs in front of him, staying as far away as possible. For a while we sit in silence, gazing at the cars churning up water as they cruise through a stream of melted snow.

"When I pass my permit test, I'll call you for driving lessons," I finally say. "You might be an astronaut by then, though."

He grins. "I'm willing to take you today. How bad can you be?"

"Honestly? I'm terrible. Just sitting behind the wheel scares me."

"What's so scary? Can you steer? And press your foot on the gas pedal?"

"You mean at the same time?"

"Okay, forget I offered."

"No, wait." Before he abandons me, I scoot closer and circle my fingers around his wrist, feeling his pulse jump. "I need to conquer this irrational fear. I want to hit the open road."

"How about hitting the back of the Towne Shopping Center lot?" He sounds more than a little nervous.

"Behind all those the stores? Yeah, that works."

I release my grip, and for a second, I think Andy might make a run for it. But, he rises from the bench and tilts his head back in the direction we came.

"Let's do it. I'll ask Sidh to drop us off at my house."

We circle back through town and find Sidh casually window shopping in front an electronics repair shop. He's more than happy to oblige our request for a ride. Andy insists that I sit in the front seat of Mr. Eknath's huge, top of the line Cadillac. Hmm. Maybe Jana and I should aim for a ride in the Eknath mobile instead of the Altomeri hot rod. But Dom's car is so much sexier than this old man boat.

"Observe." Andy pokes his head up front and points toward the gearshift.

"Observe what?"

"Sidh's driving."

Sidh flashes me an extra-bright smile as he putters down Andy's block, looking everywhere but directly ahead. He rotates the steering wheel inch by inch, and brakes once every few houses. I'm willing to bet that the needle on the speedometer has never reached a vertical position.

"Doesn't look so hard," I say, watching Sidh expertly

engage the left turn signal. He executes a clean, precise maneuver into Andy's driveway, keeping one hand in the twelve o'clock position and the other on a can of Red Bull. Mr. Drum strongly recommends nine and three.

"Good luck, Sadie. Dude, it was nice knowing you." As soon as Andy and I step out of the car, Sidh rips it into reverse and races away. I guess the slow-motion driving was all an act.

Once the dust from Sidh's tires settles, Andy pulls a mini remote from his pocket and unlocks his car doors. "Ready to go?"

We stuff ourselves into the two-door hybrid. Andy drives to the shopping center.

"Pop quiz time," he announces as we wait at a light. "What's the speed limit on this road?"

"All residential roads in the downtown area have a twenty-five mile per hour speed limit," I recite.

"Really? Is that true?" Andy's eyebrows lift.

"It's the first thing we learned in Driver's Ed. Did you miss that day?"

"I didn't take Drum's class. I had a private instructor."

"Of course you did." I make a snorting sound and turn to gaze out the window.

"Something wrong with that?" Andy asks in an even voice. I swing my head back to look at him. Is he serious?

"Well, it's just that your dad can easily afford a

private tutor. And private flying lessons. And my dad …"
Enough said.

We bend around a side street, and the Towne Center shops appear in front of us. Andy turns into a narrow drive, winding his way behind a long line of overpriced restaurants and fancy clothing boutiques. The back alleyway houses only a few dumpsters and the occasional UPS drop shipment. The perfect track for a new driver.

Andy shifts into park, hops out, and jogs around the car. I scoot over the center console to man the steering wheel. When he lowers himself into the passenger side, his knees bump the dashboard.

"Man, you're short." He jerks the seat back in a swift movement.

"I'm five three, only one inch less than the average American female." This statistic I have committed to memory. "I'm just not freakishly tall like you."

He passes his hand over my head, as if measuring my size. "There is no way you're a hair above five two."

"Okay, maybe I'm rounding up. But I'm pretty sure I have at least one more growth spurt in me. Can we start my lesson now?"

I place my hands at ten-thirty and one forty-five, hoping Mr. Drum would approve. When we practiced on a real car in class one day, he had difficulty comprehending that for those of us with shorter, non-tattooed arms, nine and three wasn't comfortable. After hearing our protests, he loomed over us, cracking his knuckles and flexing his biceps, until we obeyed his orders.

"Move the gearshift into drive, put your foot on the gas and steer," Andy says.

"That's it?"

"Let's see if you can handle that much without a catastrophe."

"Ha-ha. Very funny." I suck in a huge breath, pull back on the gearshift and switch from park to drive.

So, maybe I hit the gas pedal a wee bit too hard.

The car rockets forward, tires burning over asphalt.

"Stop!" Andy flings his arm in front of me, preventing my head from fracturing the windshield.

By the time I hit the brakes, the air smells like charred rubber. The car slides into a crazy skid, snapping my neck backward.

Holy whiplash.

"Not so fast!" Andy hollers. "What the hell are you doing?"

"I don't know!" I throw my hands in the air. "Wait, did you just curse?"

Andy dives for the steering wheel. "Don't let go! Are you trying to get us killed?"

"Sorry! Sorry! I told you I was a terrible driver." Tears brim in my eyes and slide down my cheeks as I dissolve into a fit of hysterics. When I start hiccupping, even Andy caves to a tight grin.

"You're a complete maniac." He shakes his head from side to side. "Are you sure Evil Knievel isn't teaching your Driver's Ed class?"

"Who's that?"

"Never mind."

"Do you want to switch spots?" I ask, ready to raise the white flag.

"No. I want you to try again. You can do this."

Andy's blue eyes are clear and steady, despite his white-knuckled grip on the door handle. His right foot rests on the floor mat as if he's prepared to press on an imaginary brake pedal.

"Sure you want to risk it?"

"No. Yes. No. Just do it, before I change my mind."

So I try again. I lightly tap my foot on the gas, and the car inches forward. I panic and stomp on the brake. The car slams to a stop and our bodies ping-pong back and forth.

"Better," Andy says through gritted teeth. "Again. Stop at the next dumpster."

I start and stop four more times. Each time the car handles a little easier. Eventually, the forward and braking motions seem almost natural.

"I can drive!" I return the gearshift to park and slap

the steering wheel with both hands. "I drove somewhere. In a straight line. And I'm still alive."

"We're both still alive," Andy says, sounding pretty grateful about it.

"Thanks, Andy. You're the best!"

Without thinking, I reach my arms up and around his neck. He freezes for a second before leaning into my embrace. I inhale the scent of his guy shampoo, mingled with sweaty T-shirt smell. His clothes are still damp from playing basketball, in addition to a new layer of perspiration added within the last five harrowing minutes. He doesn't smell disgusting sweaty, though, but good sweaty, all warm and athletic.

His hand moves to my hip, as if he's considering pulling me closer. For a second I forget about all of my preconditioned Andy notions. He's not a nerd, or a genius, even. He's a guy who risked his life to teach me how to drive. A guy with gorgeous blue eyes. I rest my head on his shoulder, and my cheek rubs against his neck. Then, I actually consider turning my face and brushing my lips against his flushed skin. When this idea flashes through my mind, an icy shiver runs down my spine. I shrug away from him.

"Um, can you take me home now? And I should call Jana. I kind of deserted her after the test."

Andy nods, looking as shocked as I feel about what

just happened. He removes his hand from my hip, uncrumples his body, and jumps out of the car, while I scramble over the cup holders, back to the passenger side.

As we drive away, Andy blasts the radio to cover our stunned silence. We travel the four blocks to my apartment without making eye contact. When he drops me off in front of my building, I shout a fast good-bye and sprint toward the entryway.

I think I made a big mistake. My relationship with Andy has always been simple. He annoys me on a daily basis, and I bug the heck out of him every chance I get. Whatever just happened between us didn't feel simple.

And I hate complexity.

Fill It In – Random List
Ten More Ways to Screw Up Your Life

1. Talk to Andy.
2. Allow yourself to be alone with Andy.
3. Get into a car with Andy.
4. Let Andy teach you how to drive.
5. Try driving a car with an untrained professional just because he claims he can also fly an airplane.
6. Look directly into Andy's blue eyes.
7. Hug a sweaty guy after his basketball game. Sweat is sexy.
8. Allow yourself to be alone in a car with the person you were voted "Most Likely to Marry" when you don't even like him that way. At all. Seriously.
9. Fantasize about the person you were voted "Most Likely to Marry" and imagine ten years down the line you might actually marry him. Because you won't. See number 8 above.
10. Fall in Love with the wrong person.

Chapter Fifteen

My stomach flip-flops when I pull up Mr. Drum's website on Tuesday morning. As the screen fills in, I scan for big red Fs, but find only A's, B's and one C. Underneath his tough guy exterior, could Mr. Drum possibly possess a sense of humor? I tap the down arrow, scrolling to my student ID number. The grade listed is "A".

Stunned, I close out the site and re-type the address. The A is still there. Next, I check Jana's student ID. Her grade matches mine.

In school, we greet each other with loud whoops and a running hug.

"I never have to face Mr. Drum again," I say.

"Unless you switch one of your electives to auto shop."

She cracks a wicked grin. She highly enjoyed my driving distractions list when I recited it to her over the phone.

"Ha-ha. If you could read faster, I wouldn't have had to die of embarrassment in front of him."

"I am a slow reader," she admits. She pulls our torn Fill It In list from her backpack and flattens the creases with her hand. "Acing Driver's Ed is an awesome achievement. So, we have three items filled in. Seven more to go. Our next target area should be our social lives."

"Lack of social lives, you mean. And the prom is coming up, so I guess we need to scrounge up some dates."

Jana stuffs the list into her backpack. "Can we aim a little higher than last year?"

"Why, upright and breathing wasn't good enough?"

"Not for the senior prom. This year I want gorgeous. Heart-stoppingly handsome. Prom pictures are forever, and dresses are expensive. I'm not going all out for some guy with lousy table manners."

***

Lucky for us, on Friday afternoon I hit the social jackpot.

"Whatcha got going on this weekend, Sadie?" Dominic asks, leaning back in his chair and propping his feet on the lab table. His breath smells like Doritos. For someone who claims to be a serious athlete, he sure does like junk food.

"Nothing definite," I tell him, meaning absolutely nothing.

"Come chill with me tomorrow night, then. My parents are opening a restaurant in Atlantic City."

"A new Trattoria Altomeri?" Dom's family owns and operates the best Italian restaurant in Harmony. Unfortunately, Mom and I can't even afford the appetizers on the menu.

"Yeah, my brother finished culinary school and he's running the place. Anyway, they'll be out all night."

Although this is my first personal invite to one of Dom's parties, I pretty much know what to expect. Stories circulate around school on Monday mornings, rehashing the all-out craziness occurring whenever Dom is left home alone. Alcohol. Partial nudity. High school high jinx involving shaving cream and mud wrestling in the backyard.

Actually, from what I've heard, Dominic isn't a big drinker, and he isn't tight with the pot-smoking crowd. But he does seem to crave constant insanity as entertainment.

"I'll try to stop by," I say, playing it cool.

"You too, AK," Dom says, nodding to Andy. "We should all hang out before we go our separate ways."

"Sure, man, I'll try to make it," Andy agrees without lifting his eyes from his notebook. Since the driving lesson culminating in the two of us hugging it out, Andy and I have yet to revert back to our usual give and take bickering. We're cordial, to use a boring, grown-up word, but I feel like an invisible force field now exists between us, and breaking through will only lead to certain disaster.

In fact, if this were last week, or last year even, I would express mock amazement over Andy's response. It occurs to me that I have no idea what goes on in his social life. I've run into him at the movies with different girls or with Sidh, but to my knowledge, he's never attended an alcohol party. Most likely because, his father being who he is, Andy realizes if he's caught drinking his mug shot will be plastered on the front page of the Harmony Intelligencer. Under a headline reading *Prominent Doctor's Son Arrested*.

***

"Let me in!" Colette's fist pounds on Jana's bedroom door as we dress for Dom's party. Jana's suffering from more outfit angst than usual, hiking herself in and out of every pair of jeans she owns. I'd settled on my go-to skinny jeans, black boots and a long-sleeved black shirt with mesh cut outs hours ago.

"Why can't I go with you tonight?" Colette whines through the door as Jana pours herself into yet another pair of jeans, sucking in her breath as she fumbles with the button.

"Because, if you go out with us, then I'm responsible for you. And I want to have fun, for once in my life." Swearing under her breath, Jana shrugs on a silver beaded shirt. She musses her hair with her hands to freshen up her thick waves before stomping across the room and unlocking her door.

"Sadie, will you be responsible for me?" Colette pleads, pushing past Jana and grabbing my hand. Bringing a freshman to a senior party is never a good idea, especially the freshman daughter of a well-known attorney with a draconian code of conduct. Jana comprehends the risk of underage drinking. Colette is naive. If the police raid Dom's house, she'd probably turn herself in while the rest of us jump out the closest window.

"You know I love you, Colette, but no can do. Maybe another time."

"Like when you're twenty-one. Ben's driving us, anyway," Jana informs her as she glops on mascara and blinks at her reflection in the mirror. "He doesn't want to hang out with freshmen." Secretly, I find it hard to believe that Ben would refuse a direct request from Jana if she chose to allow her sister to tag along. My best friend is high on her power tonight.

"Oooh, Ben. Jana may finally snag herself a real boyfriend." Colette puckers her lips, contorting her face into a fishy imitation of her older sister. "Wait until he finds out that you shave your legs twice a day because you're so hairy."

Jana picks up an eyeliner pencil and holds it above her head, as if preparing to bury the sharp point in her Colette's chest. "I just don't like to be all scratchy like you are, you stinking brat."

The two of them launch into a stream of back and forth curses, mixing in French and Spanish words that one would think I'd understand after hanging out with Jana's family for so long. But I still can't wrap my ears around the flying gutter talk, so I take a seat on the bed and hunt around for some reading material. I hope Ben's not waiting outside.

The monthly quiz in Jana's latest copy of Teen People is titled "Will you still be best friends in ten years?" I dog-ear the page and make a mental note to ask Jana to fill in her answers. After World War III dies down.

A few minutes later, Mr. Rodriguez's heavy footsteps ascend the stairs to break up the catfight. Before he reaches the third floor, Colette storms out, still screaming about Jana's egomaniacal beauty regimen.

I set down the magazine. "How does Colette know about Ben? Did I miss something?"

Jana paces the room, still muttering trash talk. "Ben?" She smiles, as if his name is a magic word snapping her out of an evil spell. "Oh, right. Because she's a nosy brat. She borrowed my phone after her battery died and went through my messages. Sorry, I didn't tell you, but I didn't want to upset you. He texts a few times a day."

"A few times a *day*?"

Jana grins and grabs the nearest canopy post for balance as she steps into her boots. "Just to say hey. Checking in, mostly."

"And why would that upset me?"

She looks up at me. "Because no one is texting you?" I note the way she carefully phrases the statement to sound like a question.

"Do you think I want you to be unhappy, even if I die alone?"

Jana consumes herself with a stuck zipper on her boot. "No."

"Guys have texted you to say hey before, and you've always felt the need to update me."

"You're right. But this could be …"

"Different?" I ask. "He could be the one?"

"No, not the one," Jana says, unconvincingly. "But,

he could possibly stick around for more than six weeks."

Yikes. Jana's on the verge of shattering her dating record.

"Good for you. At least one of us is getting somewhere with social achievements." I toss the magazine on the bed and wrap her into a fierce hug.

I'm happy for her.

Really. I am.

Downstairs, the doorbell rings. Show time.

"Be my shield?" Jana whispers. Over the years, I've become an expert at providing cover for her. I run down the stairs and excitedly greet Ben like he's my date. Ben looks confused, so before he spits out any revealing information, I grab his arm and drag him past Mr. Rodriguez, who's waiting to launch into a parental inquisition. Jana breathes a sigh of relief as she follows a few steps behind. Outside, I hop in the back of Ben's family minivan, and Jana sits shotgun, nervously fiddling with the radio and shifting around in her seat, an ultra-wide smile painted on her face.

So, Ben must text Jana more than he talks to her, because it's a quiet ride through town. When we stop at a traffic light, Ben's gaze drifts Jana's way, as if his eyes aren't completely under the control of his brain. I wonder if Jana senses his level of interest. If she did, my guess is that she wouldn't be acting like she'd swallowed a handful of her Grandma's happy pills.

I settle back into the bench seat, fading into the dark. Hopefully, a few drinks will loosen Ben up and he'll admit his true feelings. I know better than to expect him to fall to his knees and profess undying love, but at some point he needs to move beyond the sad puppy dog eyes or even someone as date-challenged as Jana will lose interest.

Ben angles into a parking spot a few blocks north of Dom's house, camouflaging the van between two similar family vehicles in the event police cruise through town in search of underage perpetrators. My heels dent the grass as we dash through the Altomeri's neighborhood, stopping at Dom's back door, where a handwritten sign informs us that tonight's festivities are strictly BYOB.

"Did Dom tell you to bring your own drinks?" Jana asks as we nudge our way through throngs of drunken friends greeting us with the Harmony High fight song. Apparently, it's spirit night at Dom's house. And the sign on the door hasn't deterred the rest of our senior class from keeping poor Dom company.

Over a rousing second verse of the anthem I holler, "He didn't mention anything."

"No worries," Ben says, unzipping the gym bag he'd carried in. "I brought a six pack. Here." Jana and I each crack open a beer. The bitter smell mixes with a cigarette stench hanging in the air, wreaking havoc on my sensory system. My vision fogs, blurring the scene in front of me.

"Cheers to Ben," Jana says, clanking her can against mine. We take long sips, knowing we have a long way to go to catch up with everyone partying around us.

"Cool, Sadie's here." Dom staggers into the kitchen, grabs my hand, and tows me along with him. He tosses his empty bottle into a recycling bin. With both hands free, he locks me in a bear hug. "You look amazing."

My face grows warm at his compliment even though I know it's a booze-fueled statement. We cling to each other a little too tightly and a little too long. His excuse is the fact that he's stinking drunk. I have no excuse other than my inability to suppress a desire to remain up close and personal to his kick ass abs. The ultra-toned, rock hard abs I've sat next to for over two months now.

Post-shameless-hug, Dom snakes his arm around my waist and pulls me further away from Jana and Ben. Everyone in the kitchen quits talking and watches us go by. As soon as Dom realizes we have an audience, he kisses the top of my head, probably because it's the closest part of my body to his lips. I breathe in the reek of alcohol and his cologne, strong enough to function as smelling salts if I happen to pass out.

"I want to show you something," Dom says, his words sounding slurry. "It's upstairs. In my room."

I gulp. "Uh, okay." I telegraph a look of panic to Jana,

but she only smiles and rolls her eyes.

Before I have time to formulate a list of the potential consequences of my actions, Dom leads me through a marble-tiled foyer with fresco painted walls, then up and around a spiral staircase. The second floor of the house is pitch dark.

"So, um, what do you want to show me?" I latch on to the top of the railing, torn between racing away or letting this scenario play out the way I'd dreamed about for years. Dom raises a finger to his lips, then throws open the nearest door and yanks me inside a cramped closet. The smell of feet makes me cough and sputter. It's like a shoe graveyard in here, with stacks of track spikes, baseball cleats, and Nike high tops.

"We're alone. Cool, huh?" Dom says. Okay, so maybe I truly am the stupidest person in the history of the universe, but, honestly, I expected more from Dom than seventh-grade games like spin the bottle and lock yourself in a closet with a member of the opposite sex.

I lean against the door, needing a second to think about what's happening. But, before I move out of reach, Dom wraps his arms around me and crushes his lips on mine. His hands roam over the top of my shirt, dangerously close to areas I don't consider open for business on a first hook-up.

For a second, I freeze, unsure how to react. Then, I

place my arms on his chest, holding him at bay while trying not to recoil from the taste of stale tobacco. When he finally extracts his tongue from my mouth, his hands travel down to my waist. As he sways back and forth, I clutch the front of his T-shirt, fearing I may wind up flattened like a pancake underneath him.

"This was an experiment. I wanted to see what would happen if I found myself alone in the dark with my lab partner," he explains, sounding way too logical for someone having trouble dealing with the effects of gravity.

"Oh," I say, wishing I had one hand free to wipe his saliva from my lips.

"It wasn't great, was it?" he asks with a smug grin.

"To be honest, it was kind of like kissing my brother. If I had a brother," I admit.

"You're funny. I like that in a girl." He relaxes his grip on me and kicks open the closet door. "See ya, sis." Taking the stairs two at a time, he disappears into the crowd, anxious to move on with his evening, I guess.

"What happened?" Jana asks in a low voice when I find her in the kitchen.

"He kissed me," I say, touching my still-puffy lips.

"I knew it! Was it awesome?" Any semblance of volume control disappears from Jana's voice.

"Surprisingly, it really wasn't," I say, still dazed. "There was a lot of slobber. Do you have any breath mints?"

She reaches into her pocket and pulls out a tin of Altoids. "Always."

As Jana continues chugging beer, I pop three mints in my mouth and wince at the harsh taste. It's like scraping an ultra-fresh Brillo pad across your taste buds.

"Ooh Sadie, you know what, we can make this kissing Dom thing some type of achievement."

"Like what? Kissing a hot guy? I hope that isn't a once in a lifetime event."

"Yeah, you're right. I don't want to jinx ourselves." She taps her finger on her chin, thinking. "How about kissing two boys in one night?"

"Great. Go kiss Ben and we'll add it to our list."

"What? Me kiss Ben? That doesn't count."

"Why? You want to kiss someone else?"

"No, I meant one of us kisses two guys in one night. At the same party." Jana's brows knit as she ponders the possibilities. "Or both of us kiss two guys in one night. At the same party. Hah. Like that would ever happen!"

My head starts to spin, not solely from the cloud of smoke in the room or the two sips of beer I drank before Dom dragged me away.

Jana glances at Ben, who's standing with a group of guys from the track team. "I can't really push him. We only started texting a few weeks ago."

"At least you've had digital discussions," I say. "You're asking me to kiss a total stranger!"

"It's a party. Everyone knows kissing at a party is meaningless. Just about any guy here would be glad to help us out, if we told him it was for a *thing*."

"Everyone here just saw me go upstairs with Dom. I don't want people to think my *thing* is acting like a slut."

Jana shrugs and sloshes the last few drops of beer around in her can. "School's over in a few months. No one cares about their reputations anymore. Just have fun."

At that very minute, the back door smacks open and a tall form strolls into the kitchen. I strain my eyes, taking in a short crop of blond hair. My knees begin to cave as Andy Kosolowski slides into focus, with a new haircut, minus his eyeglasses. He's wearing a tight shirt skimming over muscles I'd never imagined existed under his god-awful sweats. And his dark jeans are even more flattering than the corduroy pants that threw me for a loop in Market Fresh.

"Holy Geez-us," I say.

Jana follows my gaze and does a drastic double take. "Who is that?" she asks. "Does Andy have a hot twin brother on break from military school?"

I shake my head and bump my fist against my chest to restart my heart. "No. That's Andy."

"Wowee. Did he hire a personal shopper?" Jana slaps my arm, breaking me out of my stupor. "You were right Sadie; he is like Clark Kent. Superman in the house!" She points to Andy, who's thankfully engrossed in conversation with Sidh. I continue to stand there like an idiot, my mouth hanging open.

"Chica, you're staring." Jana leans over and whispers in my ear.

"Sorry. I just …" I'm at a total loss.

"Um, you may not want to hear this, Sadie, but Clarkie over there's probably your best option if you want to try the double kissing achievement. He just walked in, so he missed round one of your *thing*. Just tell him how much you've wanted to be with him the last twelve years, and maybe the whole senior superlative mix-up was fate, blah, blah, blah. Maybe we can even steal someone's beer and give it to him. You know, soften him up a little."

Unfortunately for me, Jana's beer-infused rationale makes complete sense. Other than the last ten minutes of my life, I have never attracted guys for casual, impulsive kisses. And, for whatever reason I suspect Andy will, in fact, indulge my request. Given the opportunity, of course. But is this something I really want to do?

"What exactly constitutes kissing?" I need to make sure I carry through with the minimum requirement for the proposed achievement. No more, no less. "Like if

Andy and I happen to bump into each other and our lips touch …"

Jana shakes her head. "Both parties need to fully engage. And there's a three-second rule."

"What, like when you pick food up from the floor after you drop it?"

"God, no. Floor food is a five-second rule. Kissing is only three. Close your eyes, aim for Andy's mouth and count one, one thousand, two, one thousand, three, one thousand. Then disembark and say adios, amigo."

"So, I have to touch his lips for three full seconds?" My stomach jumps at the thought. "I went to detention, and now you want me to touch Andy's lips for three seconds?"

"Well, it's just that, I think you have the better shot at this one," she stammers. "If you do this, I'll work harder to do something spectacular, I promise."

"Fine. You are so breaking a law in the very near future!" I grit my teeth and stomp off in Andy's direction.

Even with his highly improved appearance, he looks uncomfortable, leaning back against the kitchen counter, hands firmly entrenched in his pockets. He seems lost, and I resist the urge to ask if he needs help finding a man in a uniform to call his mommy. Andy's definitely not a regular at Dom's parties.

"Hey, Sadie," he says hesitantly when I approach in a stalkerly manner.

"Hey, Andy. What happened to your hair? And your glasses?"

"I, ah, got a haircut. And I'm trying out new contacts. My flight instructor recommended them for vision correction."

"Cool. How about another driving lesson?"

"Are you drunk?" he asks, suspiciously.

"Stone cold," I say, crossing my heart. "Jana and I are merely observing the festivities."

"Okay. Let me just tell Sidh," he says. "In case you hit a wall or something and I wind up with amnesia."

I get the idea that he isn't joking.

"Not gonna happen," I promise. "Send Sidh in Jana's direction. She'll entertain him until we get back." My best friend deserves payback for putting me through this.

Andy and Sidh exchange a few brief words, which, based on their body language appears to be some sort of a pep talk. Sidh waves to me and flashes a huge grin, wordlessly thanking me for taking Mr. Nervous Nelly off of his hands for a while.

When Andy returns, I cut and run through the kitchen door, for once leaving him struggling to keep up as I vanish into the dark February night. At the first intersection I stop, pretend to shiver and lean into him. His tall body stiffens for a second, registering my uncharacteristic sign of affection, and then he drapes a long arm around my shoulders.

"Thanks. It's cold out here." I smile up at him, injecting coyness into my expression. What I wouldn't give for just one beer in my system. Ben's donated can somehow disappeared when I left with Dom.

"You're not really dressed for the weather," he says, and his long fingers brush over one of the cutouts in my shirt, igniting a trail of heat along my bare skin. "What happened to you?"

"What do you mean?"

"You have holes in your clothes. Did you have an accident?"

I lock my jaw to stop my teeth from chattering and press into him for added warmth. "No accident. It's a fashion statement."

"What's your statement? Are you conserving natural resources by wearing less material?"

"Exactly. I'm eco-friendly." When I bat my eyelashes, his Adam's apple bobs up and down.

"My car is this way," he says, his voice cracking. We find his vehicle wedged into a tiny street spot. I leap past him into the driver's seat.

"Why don't you at least let me pull out?" Andy asks, and I hear another nervous hiccup in his voice.

"C'mon, buddy, give a girl a chance." His shoulders drop and with a sigh, he relents. When he lowers himself in the passenger side, I turn to him.

"How do I start this thing?"

"You know, Sadie, it's dark, and you're not the best driver in broad daylight, so maybe …"

"What? You're backing out of this?" I infuse anger into my voice.

Andy closes his eye and presses his fingertips into his temples. "I'll still take you driving. Tomorrow, maybe?"

"Fine. Then you owe me something for making me walk outside in this bitter cold!" I am resoundingly irate. I'm not starring in the school musical for nothing, dammit.

"What do you want?" he asks, eyeing me warily.

"I want—this." I suck in a huge breath and dive over the center console, smashing my lips against his. Of course, kissing him is even worse than kissing Dominic.

Because it's a good kiss.

Better than good.

Once Andy catches up with the program and realizes what's going on, he eases his arm around my waist and gently lifts me closer. The touch of his lips sends warmth zinging down to my toes and I forget about the cold. A small shudder runs through his body, and I can tell he's shocked out of his mind, even more surprised than I was with Dominic. But then Andy really gets into it and, in a momentary lapse of sanity, so do I.

Keeping my mouth attached to his, I scoot into his lap. My heartbeat revs up and all I can think about is touching and kissing Andy. He's hands down a better kisser than Dom. If there was a list of best kissers in the Sadie and Jana repertoire, Andrew Kosolowski would absolutely be rated number one.

When his hand slides around to the small of my back, I throw my arms around his neck, suction cupping myself to his chest, seeking more of his body heat because we never bothered to actually start the car and turn on the heater. The only sound between us is the rise and fall of our ragged breathing.

When a horn beeps at the far end of the street, we spring apart as if a bolt of lightning zapped the car.

"We should probably get back to the party," I say, shifting my weight off of him and pressing my back against the dashboard.

"Okay," he answers, robotically. His blue eyes glaze over.

"Are you all right?"

He blinks. "Okay," he says again.

I place my hands on the sides of his face and direct his head downward, checking for over-dilation of his pupils. Wait, is that just for head injuries? What happens to people who've been kissed senseless?

"Andrew. Can you say something besides okay?"

"Not right now."

"Funny. Come on, let's go." Using the toe of my boot, I pop open the passenger side door, and we topple out of the car. Andy lands in the wet grass, and I fall on top of him with a bone-jarring thud. He grunts, and I feel his chest cave in beneath me.

"Sorry. Are you hurt?" I mumble into his shoulder.

"Fine. Heh, heh."

His lunatic Kermit the Frog laugh echoes in my ears, sending me into a full-fledged panic. I scramble to my feet, ankles turning and high heels wobbling. As soon as I'm balanced, I tear away from him, back toward Dom's house.

I just kissed Andy Kosolowski. Not only that, I made a total fool of myself by jumping his bones. Like some desperate freshman girl who's never been alone with a boy.

"Do you need help, miss?" A police officer rounds the corner and steps in front of me, the brass badge pinned to his uniform gleaming in the moonlight.

I glance around, searching for Andy, but he's not close by. "No, sir. I'm walking home."

"Young women should never travel alone at night. Even a town as safe as Harmony can be dangerous." He leans in; I assume to sniff for illegal substances. I know my clothes smell like cigarette smoke, but at least no one had been drunk enough to spill beer on me. I hope Andy has the sense to hide.

"I'm walking her home, Sergeant Peters."

No, he doesn't. Super. We're both getting arrested.

"Kosolowski, right?" the officer asks. Poor Andy. Everyone in town recognizes him.

Andy comes up behind me and takes my hand. "Sadie and I were babysitting for Mr. and Mrs. Ryan. They live on Magnolia Drive." He gestures to the street behind us.

Sergeant Peters takes stock of Andy's untucked shirt, now streaked with mud, and smirks. "Say, you kids didn't happen to hear of any underage drinking going on tonight, did you? We got a tip call, and I promised to take a walk around the neighborhood."

"No, sir," I answer. "I didn't hear about anything like that." I twist my fingers through Andy's, partly to keep up appearances, partly because I'm terrified, but mostly because I don't want to let him go.

"And you're going straight home now, correct?"

"Yes, sir," Andy promises.

"Alrighty, then. Have a nice evening." Sargent Peters tips his cap and continues down the block.

"You know him?" I whisper once we've turned the corner.

"His kids are patients of my father's. And his daughter Isabel dances with my little sister. I drive the two of them to ballet class sometimes."

Just for that, I consider kissing Andy again. "Thank God you are such an upstanding citizen," I say, squeezing his hand. "I thought I'd be calling my mom to pick me up at the station."

Hands linked, we walk back to Dom's house, which by now is fully illuminated, like a three-story beacon on the edge of a dark sea. He might as well put up a sign welcoming the entire population of Harmony, PA to his drink fest. Oh, yeah, he did that too.

Right as we reach the front porch, Andy tugs me back.

"Sorry. Do I have your key?" I ask, fumbling in my jeans' pockets.

"No. We never got to the actual driving part." As he speaks, his hands rest lightly on my hips. His eyes sparkle in the moonlight and the expression on his face tells me what's next. His ridiculous height is so out of synch with my less than average stature that he needs to bend way down when he kisses me. I rise on my tiptoes and lay my hand on his chest, feeling his heartbeat quicken.

We're in danger of losing ourselves in another long, drawn out make-out session when the front door springs open, and someone tumbles down the porch steps into a line of manicured boxwoods. After several loud gagging coughs, I hear the unmistakable sound of barf in action.

"Good job Dumbchuck," Ben calls, poking his head outside.

"Gross," I say.

Ben lifts his eyes from Dom and points my way. "Aha. Another victim of the Dumbchuck."

"Another victim? Does he do this a lot?"

"Dom has the weakest stomach known to man. He'll reverse gears after track races, three sips of beer or at the sight of baby pigs. Hey, what are you two doing out here?" Ben's eyes narrow suspiciously.

"Just talking," I say and step away from Andy.

"Sure you were," Dom's voice rises from the depths of the mulch.

"Shut up, Altomeri," Andy says. "I'm going back inside. It stinks out here."

"And, Ben, you may want to switch off a few lights and take the 'come in and arrest all of us' sign off the door. There's a cop roaming the neighborhood," I say.

After the abrupt end to our supposed driving lesson, I swiftly part ways with Andy inside Dom's house. I drag Jana away from what was surely an enthralling conversation about the math portion of the SATs with Sidh and tell her we need to leave.

"Andy and I ran into a cop outside, and he's looking for an underage party to raid."

"I need to find Ben," she says.

"Forget Ben. He's babysitting Dom."

She grabs my arm, suddenly remembering where I've been. "What happened with Andy?"

"Mission accomplished. Quite an achievement, huh?" I grin stupidly. Jana probably thinks I'm happy about the *Fill It In* list, but really I just can't get the excitement of being with Andy out of my head. I'm beginning to believe in fate. Maybe Andy and I are meant to be together.

Fill It In – Your Awesome Achievements
To Be Completed By Sadie Matthews and Jana
Rodriguez Prior to June 1ˢᵗ

1. Break a School Rule — Sadie & Jana Cut Homeroom!
2. Serve My First Detention — Sadie
3. Star in the School Play — Sadie & Jana are Audrey II
4. Pass Driver's Ed — Sadie & Jana
5. Kiss Two Boys in One Night — Sadie
6.
7.
8.
9.
10.

Chapter Sixteen

"Monday morning status update." Jana pulls out the official copy of our Awesome Achievements list and flattens the wrinkled paper on top of her Spanish binder. I slam my locker door closed and try to push all thoughts of Andy from my head. He's been permanently stuck in my brain since Saturday night.

Jana uses her pencil to tick off items. "Awesome, we're halfway done."

"And a few more IP."

"Say what?"

"In process."

"Oh. Right. Do you think we should record the actual date of each event?"

I glance around, searching for Andy. He usually makes an appearance in the senior hallway before homeroom. When I turn my attention back to Jana, I notice she's looking at me funny.

"Are you still sleepy? I asked you about writing down the dates."

"Oh. Sorry. I recorded the date we skipped homeroom in my journal if you need it."

"Text me tonight. Now that we passed Driver's Ed, when are we taking our permit tests?"

"After spring break. Between track and *Little Shop of Horrors* practice we can't waste two hours waiting in line at the DMV." Further down the hall, a tall head pokes up above the crowd. I push back a glimmer of disappointment when I realize it's just a sophomore on the basketball team.

"What's next, do you think?" Jana's asking me.

"You need a solo achievement. I have two already. Any ideas?"

"Would kissing someone in front of the school sign count?"

"Who, shy Ben? If you can talk him into kissing you in front of school, it definitely counts."

"Yeah, but we're still just friends," Jana responds, a little crankily.

After Dom had finished retching up the contents of

his stomach last Saturday night, he passed out cold on the marble floor. We all stepped over him on our way out, leaving Ben to tackle clean up duty alone. He also wound up spending the night at Dom's to make sure his friend survived the effects of binging. Meanwhile, Jana and I froze our butts off taking a roundabout route home on foot. Luckily, I didn't run into Sergeant Peters again while milling around town close to curfew, smelling like pure guilt.

"What about detention?" she moves on before I continue to question her about Ben. "Do you have that date in your journal?"

"No. I couldn't bring myself to write about the experience. But I'll never forget it."

"Good enough. And did you ever ask Dom about a ride in his car? After Saturday night … "

"After Saturday night when I told him he kissed like my brother?"

Jana makes a pained face. "Ouch. Okay, I can work on that one. I have some ideas."

"Do you, now?"

She smiles a Mona Lisa smile, revealing nothing. "Our latest and perhaps greatest achievement is all thanks to you. Two boys snogged." She pencils in the victims' names and Saturday's date. "I can add the times too. Say around ten p.m. and ten fifteenish?"

"Somewhere around there," I agree.

"Fantastic. We're some making decent progress overall. Here, why don't you just take this home tonight and pencil in your dates for detention and homeroom cutting?" She hands the list to me. I shove it between my class binders. "I'm sure both boys would be happy to testify on your behalf. Maybe they've even recorded the experience on the bathroom wall."

"Funny. So, about Ben –"

"Morning, ladies." A familiar voice interrupts our conversation. Whirling around, I find Andy approaching us, smiling from ear to ear. His new haircut and lack of glasses still throws me for a loop, and I momentarily lose track of all my other thought processes in the midst of gawking.

"Girl talk, Andy," Jana says, less impressed by his new look. "Keep walking." She indicates with her index and middle finger what his legs should be doing.

"Yeah, leave, Andy," I say, but my voice sounds shrill and weak. I'm stuck on this Kosolowski metamorphosis. Scientists should name a butterfly after him or something.

"That's not what you were saying Saturday night, right, Sadie?" His smile spreads wider, if possible, leaving me torn between hyperventilation and drooling.

"I don't recall us having much of a conversation at all," I say, locking my eyes with his.

"Because I stunned you into silence," he says, and I laugh.

"Gosh. Look at the time. Gotta go." Jana glances at her non-existent wristwatch. When she turns away, her backpack bumps my elbow. I let out a yelp. All of my morning work drops to the floor.

"Oops. See ya," she calls out, vanishing around the corner, not bothering to help me pick up the mess.

When I crouch down to collect my junk, I spy a familiar looking wrinkled paper under Andy's right high top.

"I've got it. Hey, relax, Sadie," Andy says, sensing my desperation. He bends down and grabs the list. "What's this? A love letter to your secret obsession?"

"Give it, Andy. Now." I dive for the paper but miss. He straightens up to skyscraping heights. I pounce on him with the speed of a hungry tiger. Laughing, Andy holds the paper high above his head where I have no hope of reaching it. Unless I jump. Like a kangaroo on steroids, I spring up and down. But I miss. And I miss again. And again.

"Fill It In – Your Amazing Achievements," Andy announces to those of us left in the hallway, meaning the two of us. "Number 1. Break a School Rule — Sadie and Jana Cut Homeroom. Is that why you wanted to skip? Stupid me, I thought you just wanted Dom to pay attention to you."

"Zip it, Andrew." My voice shakes as I swipe with my arm again, but Andy lifts the paper above his head and squints at Jana's loopy combination of cursive and block print.

"Number 2. Serve My First Detention. Completed by none other than Sadie Matthews, who shouted a curse word in the biology lab. Number 3. Star in the School Play. Ah, yes, the plant. You're kicking ass with this, aren't you?"

"Give it to me now or I will kill you!" I amp up the venom into my voice and claw at him, digging my fingernails into his shirt. He doesn't flinch. He must have skin of steel. Maybe he really is Superman in disguise.

The homeroom bell rings.

"C'mon, Andy. We're going to be late." I desperately appeal to his over-conscientiousness, but Andy ignores me as he continues to read down the list. His ears, plainly visible thanks to his shorter haircut, turn bright red. I can't tell if he's angry, embarrassed, or both, but whatever emotion flows through him right now, I'd bet it's not a good one. After what seems like hours of deafening silence, he clears his throat with one long, painful-sounding scrape of his vocal chords.

"Please give it to me, Andy," I whisper.

He extends his long arm. "Glad to be of service," he says. Then he fakes me out and drops the paper on the ground. I trash every last shred of my dignity as I dive for the list, crinkle it into a ball and run.

***

So, calculus is fun. Andy's sneaker taps out a maddening rhythm while he frenetically works on functions. I consider stomping my heel on his big toe, but that would be cruel. Plus, I'm on the verge of crying, for some reason. I can't tell if the tears burning in my eyes are real, or if I'm unconsciously making a play for sympathy. Probably a little bit of both.

After allowing us thirty minutes to complete independent work, Mrs. McCaffrey launches into a new unit.

"After working through these four steps, you can easily solve for x," she says a few minutes later. "Does anyone have the answer yet?"

Total cricket job. The entire class must wear matching zombie expressions, because when Mrs. McCaffrey glances around, she counts exactly zero volunteers. After a minute, she calls on her go-to problem solver. And guess what—for the first time ever, Andy Kosolowski gives an incorrect answer.

Mrs. McCaffrey's jaw drops. She checks the equation on the board. "Are you feeling okay, Andy?"

"Um, sorry, I calculated the cosecant, not the cosine," he mumbles. Mrs. McCaffrey sighs, assigns us all extra homework, and ignores her star pupil for the rest of the period.

***

"Emergency meeting!"

"What happened? Did Dominic chuck up his breakfast on you?" Jana asks when we meet in front of the cafeteria for lunch.

"No. Our list has been compromised!"

"What do you mean, compromised?" Her dark eyes seem to grow to three times their normal size. "Are we getting kicked out of school for cutting homeroom?"

"We haven't been expelled—yet. But Andy read our achievements."

"You showed the list to Andy? Have you lost your mind?" Jana grabs my wrist and pulls me out of the lunch line.

"Of course I didn't show it to him! It's your fault— you bumped into me when you ran away this morning, and I dropped it. Andy trapped it under his submarine sized foot and then used his extra-long arms to hold it away from me while he read it."

"Ha! You're so busted." Jana smirks as she releases her hold on me.

"*We're* so busted, you mean."

"Did he read number five?"

"Yes, he read number five, right along with his name and Dom's name, which you so kindly filled in."

Jana giggles, still thinking this is funny. "Did he laugh?"

"No, Jana. He failed to find even one lousy shred of humor in the situation."

"Uh-oh. Maybe he was laughing on the inside?" Jana finally gets the picture.

"Not at all. He threw the list on the ground. By the time I picked it up, he was gone."

Jana hands me a lunch tray before grabbing one for herself. "What if he tells Dom? You sit between them in class. They'll be comparing notes and not just biology notes. I mean, not just biology class notes."

"Got it, Jana. Hilarious. I don't know why you had to go and tell me to kiss him, anyway."

Jana stops dead in the center of the crowded cafeteria. I flip my empty tray up against my chest before it smashes into her back.

"Was it so terrible to kiss two guys? I thought we both agreed it would be an amazing achievement."

"It was a stupid decision. I have a hard enough time managing one boy. Why did I think I could handle two?"

We silently pace along the salad bar. I pass on the wilted lettuce and head for the grill.

As the deep fryer sizzles, Jana speaks again. "You know what, I never asked about your kiss with Andy because I assumed it was a non-event. But on the off chance that my assumption was completely off the mark—do you want to tell me about it?"

I toss a large order of cheese fries on my green plastic tray.

"It was good, wasn't it?" She grabs a carton of chocolate milk. "And now you like him, don't you?"

"Andy Kosolowski is the most annoying person on the planet," I grumble.

"Is he also the best snogger on the planet?"

My shoulders fall. "Doesn't matter now. He thinks I only kissed him because of the list."

"Why else would you kiss him? You always talk about how annoying he is. You were ready to drop out of school over the Senior Superlative thing. And you're always saying you don't want to get involved with someone and end up like your mom."

"I never said I wanted to get involved with him, did

I? Why don't you go sit with Ben?"

Jana does a double take. "Why would I want to sit with Ben?"

"Because you're totally into him. And while you're over there, figure out some way to get him to make a move. You talk big about taking risks, Jana, but I'm the one screwing up my life for a stupid list, not you." I head toward an empty chair at the stage crew table.

***

After the morning's events, I seriously consider coming down with a case of the flu before last period. But I refuse to act like a coward. At some point, I need to face Andy. And Dominic, too.

I wait in the hallway. When the bell rings, I blow into the room, heading directly to my seat.

"Hey, Sis," Dominic says. I guess the alcohol in his body hadn't caused him to black out the closet escapade. Glancing over at Andy, then back to me, Dom coughs out a harsh laugh. He must also remember what happened in his front yard right before planting his face in the hedge.

"Hey, Dom," I say, opening my binder and holding it upright. After a minute of silence, I peek around my makeshift shield to spy on Andy, and find him twirling a pencil between his fingers, staring off into the stratosphere. When he flicks a glance my way, I force a friendly, please don't be mad at me, smile. His blue eyes bore into me until I shift my gaze back to my notes.

"What's up his ass?" Dominic asks. "Dude, did Sadie hold out on you too?"

"Oh, no, I got plenty," Andy says. "Way more than I wanted."

Dominic bursts into knee-slapping laughter, along with everyone else seated in a four lab table radius.

"Did I miss something?" Dr. Brownstein says, turning his attention away from the SMART Board.

"You missed an epic weekend, Dr. B.," says Dom.

"Did you blow something up, Mr. Altomeri?"

"Nope. But I puked again."

"Stupendous! Puking is a strong indicator of high school enjoyment." Dr. Brownstein's lizard lips curve into a tight smile. "And since the vomiting occurred outside of my lab, I'm happy as well."

Fifty torturous minutes later, class is finally over. I strategically position myself in Andy's way as I pack up my binders, working up the nerve to deal with him.

"Can you move?" he asks.

"Why are you so angry?" I plant my hands on my hips. "It's not like we were going out and I cheated on you."

A heavy sigh escapes from the bottom of his chest. "I'm not mad, Sadie. I just don't like you anymore."

"Here's a piece of news, Andy. You never did like me."

Andy smiles a sad smile and his blue eyes dim. "No, see, that's where you're wrong. I pretended not to like you because it was funny. But you pretended to like me and, you know what, I didn't find that funny."

I shake my head, straining to process. What did he just say? "Andy, you're too smart for your own good. Maybe you need to sign up for a seminar on understanding what is and isn't funny instead of going to those extra physics classes you like so much."

"Sure. I'm the one who needs help understanding our situation."

"What situation? We don't have a situation!"

"Right. No situation. Enjoy the rest of high school, Sadie. I hope you find another idiot to play your immature games."

And with a disgusted shake of his head, he leaves me in his wake.

Fill It In – March 10th
Top Ten Anger Management Tips

1. Go for a walk.
2. Go to track practice and actually run.
3. Polish off a full carton of Chunky Monkey Ice Cream.
4. Lock yourself in your room and play sad love songs over and over.
5. Ignore your best friend's fifty texts.
6. Go shoe shopping.
7. Cry. A lot. It's cathartic.
8. Pull out your script and try to get into the character of a man-eating plant, wishing you really could deal with life's little problems by feeding them to obnoxious alien foliage.
9. Pull out your last eleven yearbooks and deface Andy's pictures by scribbling facial hair all over them.
10. Suck it up, because deep down you know you have no one to blame but yourself.

Chapter Seventeen

After my showdown with Andy, I get angry, as Coach Jenkins likes to say. My legs achieve an unprecedented rate of speed, and my split times cross into competitive territory. Coach clocks me sprinting down the hallway, he shakes his head in astonishment and hands me a baton. I'm assigned the second leg of the B relay team. Not much amazing achievement potential, given that our A team was last year's state champ. But hey, it's a real race.

"Hold up, Sadie," Dom calls when I motor by, wrapping up my final circuit. He flexes his chiseled arms, slick with perspiration. When I slow my pace, I see exactly how much sweat drips off of him. Yuk.

He drops into a set of sit-ups, showcasing his core strength, a term Coach Jenkins throws around on a daily basis. Of course, in relation to me, Coach usually talks about my lack thereof and follows up his comment with the suggestion of a daily abdominal routine including 1,000 crunches. I only wish I had that much dedication.

Dom's dark eyes meet mine between curls. "So, what'd you do to AK? He looks like he wants to put his fist through a wall every time he sees you."

"We kissed. Same as you and me. And you still like me, right?"

"Sure I do." Dom grunts his way through five more reps. "Maybe we need to try it again. I might have missed something the first time."

My stomach churns up some serious bile at the thought of reliving the stunt he pulled in his closet. No way. "You know what, maybe I'll check in at mathletes and see if I've missed anything lately." I jog down the hall in the direction of Mrs. McCaffrey's room, leaving Dominic looking sort of pissed off at my rejection. The door is closed, but I hear muffled voices, so I rap my knuckles on the frosted pane.

"Come in," Mrs. McCaffrey calls. She and Jana are engaged in a pow-wow around the teacher's desk. Between them sits a sea of math books, red plastic cups crammed with pencils, protractors, rulers, and a stack of tests waiting for grades. Mrs. McCaffrey is an anti-perfectionist mathematician who only straightens up her piles of junk when Principal Dailey visits her room during his annual observation period.

Jana turns toward me, her mocha-colored eyes watery.

"Sorry for interrupting." I step back into the hallway.

Mrs. McCaffrey waves me inside. "Sadie, we were just talking about you."

"I was telling Mrs. McCaffrey about how horrible I felt. Our argument was all my fault," Jana confesses, with a sniff. "I pushed you into a situation and I shouldn't have. I wanted to apologize, but what, was I supposed to follow you into the girl's locker room and force you to talk to me?"

I sigh. "It wasn't all your fault. I'm my own person. No one forced me into—the situation." I pray Jana didn't spill any specific details to Mrs. McCaffrey about what we apparently now refer to as the situation. I don't want the faculty to think I'm in the habit of randomly kissing boys like I did at Dom's party.

"I didn't realize that the situation had—extenuating circumstances," Jana answers, keeping up with the code.

"Ahem." Mrs. McCaffrey clears the air before we continue. "Listen girls, I need to make some copies in the office. Feel free to hang out in here until I get back." She waves a packet of worksheets on her way out the door.

"So, are we still friends?" Jana asks, as soon Mrs. McCaffrey leaves.

"We're always going to be friends. Did you think a stupid misunderstanding about a dumb list of meaningless achievements was going to ruin us?"

"I'm so sorry if I messed up your chance with Andy," she says, blinking back tears. "The day of the Senior Superlatives you seemed so mad about being associated with him."

I sink into the seat next to hers and sigh. "I was totally blindsided. I mean, I've known him since kindergarten. I never really looked at him as a potential boyfriend. But, at some point, I realized he's not the person I'd always assumed he was."

She nods. "I guess Andy's pretty mad right now, isn't he?"

I laugh. "Fuming."

"And the list? Are we quitting?"

"No way. We are completing ten amazing achievements before graduation, even if I have to kiss Andy's big smelly sneakers and beg forgiveness because he's the last living male on the planet."

"Would you kiss Dom again to get a ride in his car?" she asks, with a faint smile.

"Absolutely not. He just tried to pull that trick on me, and I wanted to tell him to stuff his tongue down someone else's throat. Any amazing achievement related to Dominic is now your responsibility."

Jana's face breaks out in a smile. "I guess I'd be willing to handle Dominic. For the sake of our friendship."

***

"Tomorrow's a big day," Jana remarks. We ease on down the sophomore hallway, taking a long, slow lap as we wrap up track practice. As soon as we began running together again, my split times reverted right back to turtle pace.

"What's so great about tomorrow?"

"Coach Jenkins said March fifteenth is the official kick off date for spring track. We get to run outside."

"Oh, right. On the trail around school."

"Yep. And to celebrate, I'm going to kiss Ben in front of the sign."

"You need to try something. Otherwise, you'll be a saggy old lady before he gets past texting."

"Do you think he'll come willingly like Andy did for you?"

"I'm pretty sure that if you lead, Ben will follow."

"If not, then I'm totally misreading him."

"How can you miss those big hazel eyes adoring you

every second of every day?"

Jana giggles. "Okay, here's my plan. I'll ask him to run warm ups with me. We'll loop around to the front of school. You need to distract Dominic."

"I thought we agreed Dom is off limits," I protest.

"You don't have to *kiss* him, chica. Just ask him for running pointers or something that involves taking his shirt off."

"Ah, taking off the shirt! Brilliant."

"I know, right? Then catch up with me for verification purposes."

"I don't need proof. You believed me, didn't you?"

"True. But I also saw both boys right after they kissed you."

"Did they have matching looks of satisfaction?"

"Sort of. Dominic looked like a wolf that just tore apart a squirrel. And Andy looked dazed and confused."

"Andy always looks dazed and confused," I say, with a snort.

"Yes, but he was a total loon that night. His blue eyes were all sparkly, too. He seemed drunk, but he wasn't at the party long enough to actually be drunk."

"Andy is high on life. Well, he used to be before I dared to lock lips with another boy the same night I kissed him. Like I knew Andy was even interested in anything besides a one-time hookup." But as the words pour from my mouth, guilt stabs the center of my heart. I picked up on *something* between us, but I chose to ignore the signs.

"Yeah, who would have thought Andy was crushing on you? Especially after the snowball incident. That's what twelve-year-olds do when they like someone, not guys heading off to Ivy League-caliber colleges in a few months. Anyway, you understand the plan for tomorrow, right?"

"Distract Dominic. I don't need to see you and Ben in action."

"Your decision. Maybe I'll snag a prom date while I'm at it."

"Another awesome achievement. But probably not list-worthy, since we did go to prom last year."

"Best friend, I'm sorry for ever doubting the power of us," Jana says solemnly and stops running to give me a hug.

***

The next day track practice gets off to a late start. Everyone mills around waiting for Coach to announce outdoor running assignments, so I take advantage of the confusion and casually ask Dominic to demonstrate the proper way to stretch before a race. On top of being a great runner, the guy is some type of yoga master. He dips into a runner's lunge so low he's practically doing a split. I attempt to mimic his pose, but the instant I flex my right knee, a pulling sensation creeps up the back of my leg. I stop mid-stretch, settling for what Dominic describes as a vaulted warrior pose. Good enough. I'm not interested in suffering for my sport.

By this time, Jana and Ben have disappeared, but no one else seems to notice. Coach Jenkins is caught up welcoming the varsity football team's offensive linemen. They showed up to shot put and run a few laps, hoping to shed their winter blubber before summer workouts begin.

"Start here," Coach says to the guys, reverting to two-word sentences when his first attempt at explaining the practice schedule is met with only blank expressions. "Run there." He points to the batting cages on the other side of campus. "Come back. To me." He points to himself. They nod and take off at a snail's pace.

"Girls team, run the cross country trail. Meet in the gym when you're done to work on relay handoffs," Coach says, turning towards the rest of us.

"How long is the cross country trail?" I ask.

"Three miles," says one of the twiggy shaped junior runner girls.

"Three miles?" My last sip of pre-practice Gatorade detours into my windpipe. I bend forward, coughing hard to help redirect the liquid electrolytes seizing hold of my lungs. I'd never run more than a mile during indoor practice.

"Welcome to spring training, Matthews," Coach Jenkins says, thumping me on the back and sending me into another round of near-asphyxiation. I recover in time to fall in at the back of the pack, keeping one eye on the trail and one on the lookout for Jana.

The girls' team gallops along like wild horses, rounding the first corner of the trail. Mud kicks up from the soggy ground and splatters the lower half of my legs. When we reach the straightaway in front of the school, I step off the trail, into the grass and kneel down to tie my shoe. Jana and Ben are still MIA.

After stalling as long as possible, I take off again, stretching out my strides to avoid losing sight of the girls. By the time they pass the school sign, I'm lagging far behind. My lungs recoil at the freshness of the air and the pungent scent of the pollinating trees. Inside practices conditioned me to breathing in stale dust. Right before the sign, I pause to catch my breath, knowing I'll never catch up. As I stand there, gasping for air, a large blond figure jumps out from the behind the school sign.

"Aha!"

My answering scream practically shatters glass in nearby car windows. "Andy! Are you trying to scare me to death?"

He's back to wearing glasses, and behind the thick lenses, he meets my fear with an icy stare. I back away from him, and turn to run in the opposite direction. My foot slides on a patch of muddy ground, sending me face first into the gravel.

"Ouch."

The taste of grass, wet dirt, and sweat swishes in my mouth as I lay on the ground. No one offers assistance, so I roll over, prop up to a sitting position, and pick a loose stone out of my scraped knee. Blood drips down the front of my leg.

"What are you doing here? Ow!" I scoot off the trail, aiming my backside toward a softer patch of brown grass. Pain shoots up the back of my leg in the spot that nagged me when I stretched out with Dominic.

"Expecting someone?" Andy directs a smug look my way. "Are you pretending to be lost so you can meet your secret boyfriend on the track team?"

"No, Andy. You've got it all wrong." I stretch my legs wide, trying to relieve the pain but only feel more of a burning, tearing sensation.

"Yeah, sure I do. I saw you and Dominic talking after school. You've been in love with him for the last three and a half years. You joined the track team for him. You probably planned the whole lab partner thing with Jana just to sit next to him."

I stare up at the bright blue sky, thinking how it matches the color of Andy's eyes when they do the amazing twinkling thing I'll probably never see again. Sheesh. I must have hit my head on the way down.

"Okay, I'll admit it. You foiled my evil master plan. Now I'll never achieve my dream of becoming Dominic's potential drunk hook-up target. Because that's all I really wanted out of my senior year, right?" I lift my arm above my head, reaching for him. "Can you help me up? I think I hurt something."

"Yeah, sure you did." His feet seem mammoth-sized when he steps closer. I clutch Andy's leg and hoist myself to a standing position, nearly taking him down in the process.

"Hey! What do you think you're doing?" he asks, trying to shake me off of him.

"I said I was hurt." I grimace and moan to further elaborate. "Are you going to walk me back to school or do you want to just watch me limp the whole half-mile? I can't call Dominic, the love of my life from here. And now the person everyone thinks I'm going to marry won't help me either!" Enraged by the stupidity of our discussion, I push away from Andy and hobble back along the cross-country trail, dragging my injured leg behind me.

I count ten steps before the possibility strikes me that he intends to watch me suffer the whole way back to school. I never imagined Andy having this capacity for hatred. A cry chokes me, but before I let it out, he comes up from behind and sweeps me in his arms like I'm a rag doll.

I can't resist curling my arms around him. "Wow. You're deceptively strong for such a skinny guy."

His lips press together like he's fighting not to smile. "And you're deceptively evil for such a cute girl."

"You think I'm cute?" I ask, wriggling beneath his vise-like grip.

He cranes his neck, checking out a jet flying overhead, marking the sky with a tail of white smoke. "You're not—ugly."

I poke his chest to bring his attention back to me. "If you had to rate me on a scale of one to ten, where would I be?" Curiosity kills me every time.

"Hmmm. Is one good or bad?"

"One is bad, math wizard. Ten is totally hot."

"Then I plead the fifth."

I pick my head up from his shoulder. "You think I'm a five?"

"No. I refuse to answer, because if I do, it will only get me in trouble."

"How bad-looking can I be?" I wonder aloud. "You kissed me."

"I was drunk," he says, with a grin.

I bring my face closer to his. "You were so not drunk. You were only at the party for like two minutes. Plus, there was no AOB."

"AOB?"

"Alcohol on breath. I didn't smell anything. When I hugged you after our first driving lesson, you hugged me back. Do you remember that?"

He rolls his eyes. "How could I forget? I still have nightmares about you almost crashing through my windshield."

"Sadie! Over here." Geez. Somehow Jana times her appearance to perfectly destroy the first enjoyable conversation I've had with Andy in days. Her shrill voice startles him, and he drops me like a bag of hot rocks.

"Ouch." My tailbone connects with the hard ground, jolting my spine out of alignment.

"Sorry," Andy says, sounding not the least bit apologetic. Ben and Jana round the corner, walking hand in hand along the running trail.

"Your friends can help you the rest of the way. See ya." With a wave, Andy ventures off in the direction of the student parking lot.

"What happened?" Jana manages to tear her eyes

away from Ben when she hears me groaning.

"I was running—like you were also supposed to be doing—and Andy jumped out from behind the school sign. He scared the bejeezus out of me, and I fell. Now my leg hurts. I can barely walk."

Jana and Ben hoist me up from the ground and cart me back to the Phys Ed building. When I describe my fall and the burning pain to Coach Jenkins, he shakes his head sadly.

"Hamstring," he pronounces. "You could be out for the season."

"What!?!" Jana and I cry in unison.

"I didn't even run in one race yet," I say. I glance at my best friend. The success of our high school achievement list now rests on her shoulders. She needs to step up and earn our varsity letter or all the hours we spent running in circles will be a waste. And unless she possesses a previously undiscovered talent for pole vaulting, we're completely doomed.

After delivering the bad news, Coach packs ice around my thigh and sends me on my way. Ben volunteers to drive Jana and me home. He runs to fetch his minivan, promising to meet us by the cafeteria doors while Jana acts as my human crutch, supporting me in front of my locker as I gather my homework.

"What happened, Sadie?" Mrs. McCaffrey steps out

of her classroom when she notices me limping by.

"I think I wrenched my hamstring at track practice."

"You're running track? Is that why you've cut back on mathletes?"

"Yeah. Sadie may be out for the season," Jana adds. "Looks like we're not earning any varsity letters before we graduate."

"It wasn't really ever going to happen, anyway," I say. "But at least we tried."

"If you want to earn a varsity letter, then why not stick with mathletes?" Mrs. McCaffrey asks, looking back and forth between us, confused. "If we win the first round competition and make it to the county championships, everyone on the team automatically letters."

Excitement burns in my chest. "Really? With Andy in our group, we're a lock for the first round."

"Let me get this straight." Jana holds up one finger as she works the idea through her brain. "Did you say the whole team letters, even if we individually stink at math?"

"Neither of you stinks at math," Mrs. McCaffrey says. "You may not be a pair of mathematical geniuses, like Mr. Kosolowski, but the two of you can hold your own against any other high school senior. I would never have asked you to be on the team if you couldn't do the work."

Jana whoops loudly and throws her arms around me,

almost taking me down for the third time that afternoon.

"Ouch," I wince, stumbling when my weight shifts onto my bad leg. But Jana is past caring about my personal discomfort.

"Our dream is alive, Sadie!"

"Great," I say, attempting to work up to her level of enthusiasm. "But I think I prefer running with a pulled hamstring over seeing Andy Kosolowski at mathletes practice every day."

Chapter Eighteen

On the way to my apartment, Jana's eyes are glued on Ben. She's completely forgotten about her severely injured best friend in the backseat. Holy awkwardness. She'd kill me if I poked my head between them and asked if they managed to kiss in front of the school sign. I can't bring up our achievement list in front of her current love interest. Especially not after the way Andy reacted when he found out kissing boys is part of my apparently misguided attempt to enjoy my final semester of high school.

Seriously, guys are such babies.

Like if Andy's situation was reversed and the opportunity arose for him to make out with two girls in one night, he would do the honorable thing and fully disclose all prior hooking up to female number two. And if Andy had bothered to get to the party on time, I might have kissed him first and avoided my Dominic experience altogether.

Anyway, after Ben and Jana help me up the stairs, they dump me in front of my apartment and make a run for it. I open my door and glance back to say thanks for the lift, but they're already gone. Sigh. I hop into the kitchen and refill the cold pack Coach gave me with new ice. Then I limp over to our sofa and collapse. Once my leg completely numbs, I switch to a heating pad. About an hour into the rest, ice, heat, elevate circuit, Mom's key scratches in the lock, signaling the end to my peaceful afternoon.

"Sadie! Are you hurt?" Her face turns nine shades of green when she notices my leg propped up on a stack of pillows.

"I think I strained my hamstring at track practice. I'm okay, though."

"Do I need to look at it? Because I don't know if I can." She covers her eyes with her hands.

"Mom. You work in a medical office. Don't you see sports injuries all the time?"

"Yes, but you're my child. It's different when your baby is in pain."

"I'm not a baby anymore, and I promise you, I'll be fine. But it looks like I'm off the track team."

"It's that bad? I'll call Dr. Kosolowski. Ask him what to do." Mom zigzags around the apartment like a confused mouse caught in a never-ending maze.

"No, wait. Anyone but him!" But she's already yakking away to the nighttime receptionist, demanding to speak with her boss. Dr. Kosolowski returns the page ten minutes later, and Mom hands me the phone.

"He wants you to describe your symptoms."

He must know how well my mother deals with these types of situations. I describe my pain on the meaningless one to ten scale (I give it an eight when I'm moving, otherwise a one and a half) and update him on my self-care. When he asks how the injury occurred, I mention my track practice and stretching routine, but I cover for Andy and don't rat out his rude behavior to his father.

After much lengthy discussion, Dr. Kosolowski's recommended course of action matches Coach Jenkins' instructions almost word for word. When I pass the phone back to Mom, she finally appears convinced that I managed to avoid permanent damage.

"Even though you might need to quit the team, I'm still proud of you," she says, sitting next to me on the couch. "You tried something new. And you still have the play to look forward too."

"Yeah, my costume should be ready soon. I'll be dressed as a giant green plant," I say, circling my index finger in the air.

Mom throws her head back and laughs. My part in the musical is a constant source of entertainment for her. "You know what I did for fun in high school? Nothing. Because I got pregnant. Not that I regret having you, but it did put a dent in my social life."

"Yeah, I guess midnight feedings limit your ability to party all night."

"Somewhat," she admits. "My advice is to take advantage of your free time. Do something spectacular. You never know where you're going to end up."

"I'm so happy you feel that way, Mom. Because I signed up for skydiving lessons this weekend."

Her face turns sheet white. "Really, skydiving? How … adventurous."

I force a laugh. "Kidding. One day of real track practice is all the outdoor excitement I ever need."

"Your choice, of course. I would never stop you," she says, with a shake of her head. "Should I make you chicken soup?" Mom is clueless about caring for my leg injury. It's amazing how she works alongside doctors and nurses every single day without even the slightest bit of medical practicality clicking in her brain.

"A normal diet will be tolerable," I say, just to play

with her mind.

"Huh?"

"Whatever, Mom. I'll eat anything."

We settle on a dinner consisting of of Ellio's pizza, baked to perfection in the toaster oven, and washed down with strawberry milk. As we eat, I prod my mother to continue her trip down memory lane. She and I never have heart to hearts. I mean, I add and subtract as well as any mathlete, so, knowing how old Mom is now, I can tell she got pregnant with me during senior year. But, I hesitate to ask for exact details, and she never volunteers much information.

"Was my dad your one true love? Is that why you never married anyone else?"

Mom ponders this question as she nibbles at the corner of her rectangular tile of pizza. "Maybe I thought I loved him. But marriage? No way. I was too young. And he wasn't interested in a lasting anything."

"You never talked about getting married?" I ask.

Mom meets my gaze. "We definitely talked about it. But even back then, I thought of marriage as one of the most important decisions I would ever make. Sure, it's hard to pick a fancy college or a future career, but you can always change where you go to school or work. You can't just shed your family." Mom folds her hands on top of the table. "I don't regret having you, Sadie. But, I also don't regret staying single. Your father and I went our separate ways. He moved across the country. I wish he'd kept in contact with you, but you can't force someone to be a parent." She reaches out and tucks a loose lock of hair behind my ear.

"It's okay. I'm used to just us."

She smiles a sad smile. "Doesn't make it right, though, does it? I got busy with work and raising you, and the next thing you know I'm comfortable my life. That's why I like to see you try new things. Take risks. Just try not to break any bones in the process, okay?"

***

By the next morning, I skate along with a barely noticeable limp. My mother manages to power through her anxiety over my injured hamstring (which on the outside looks totally normal, not even bruised), and wraps my leg with a new ace bandage.

I arrive at school later than usual, but Jana must have decided to dump me like a burning radish when I didn't show up on time, because she's nowhere in sight. I consider shuffling by Ben's locker, but ultimately just suck it up and rely on myself.

Seconds before the bell, Jana rushes into homeroom, looking very un-Jana like with disheveled hair and smeared lipstick. She pulls out her compact and finger-combs her hair through announcements.

We catch up on our way to first period. "You never told me about kissing Ben in front of the school sign yesterday. What happened?"

Jana lifts a shoulder. "We ran into Andy on the way to the sign, and Ben suggested we hide out in his minivan for a few minutes. He did kiss me, though."

"Yeah, that much I could tell. The dopey looks and hand holding gave it away."

"Was it that obvious?" she asks, breaking into a happy grin. "We were circling back to the sign when we saw you."

"So, shy Ben actually made a move, huh?"

"Did he ever." Jana laughs. "I nearly passed out when he did. Oh, and by the way, he asked me to go to the movies with him this weekend."

"Can you double with Dominic and get a ride in his car? Because I've been killing myself for this list, Jana, and you promised to take care of that one."

"Hey—I'm killing myself too. I'm half the plant, remember? I cut homeroom, too."

"I sat through detention! I kissed two guys! And one guy was totally gross, and the other one ..." Jana's eyes widen and she claps her hand to her mouth, masking the bottom half of her terrified expression. "Is right behind me, isn't he?"

A shadow falls over us as Andy approaches, his tall form blocking the glare from the overhead lights in the hallway.

"Am I the gross one or the one you will be insulting at a later date?" he asks as he lopes by without breaking his pace. I guess he isn't all that interested in my response.

***

Thanks to my latest inadvertent insult, I now have fossilized Andy, the huge, inert object taking up space at the lab table next to mine. A.P. Bio class equals supreme awkwardness. And just to make my day more fun, the other slice of my hot guy sandwich quickly senses the tension between Andy and me. Always in search of non-academic entertainment, Dominic decides to occupy himself by loudly reminiscing about our closet hook-up.

The minute I let my guard down, Dom jabs my side with the sharp point of his lead pencil, sending my backside airborne. I pop into the aisle, dropping to the floor to avoid a collision with Andy's elbow. By the end of class, my nerves are wound up like a rubber band ball, ready to snap. Through it all, the Andy Kosolowski fixture next to me refuses to budge. Even his mess of curls seems plastered to his head, unmoving.

Then, we march down to mathletes practice to continue our three-way, dysfunctional relationship.

For the next two weeks, the awkward routine continues. Dominic usually hangs out in Mrs. McCaffrey's room for twenty minutes, solves some problems, recites pi to the fiftieth decibel to impress the sophomore and junior girls, and then makes a show stopping exit.

On his way out the door, he likes to drop a bomb about sharing chicks with Andy. Everyone in nerdville, besides Jana and I, interprets Dom's rudeness as some kind of inside senior guy joke. They laugh at the very thought of Dom and Andy going out with the same girl. But, I'm positive that if I dare glance in the direction of our mathletes captain, I'd see steam blowing out of his red ears.

If Dom's particularly bored, he tugs my ponytail or winks at me in a bizarre fashion, first one eye twitching, and then the other. On track meet days, Dom skips mathletes altogether. Those are my favorite days. On mathelete competition days, he runs at night, after a long afternoon of algebraic lightning rounds.

Meanwhile, Jana and I juggle mathletes with *Little*

Shop of Horrors practice, but drama rarely conflicts with after-school activities. Ms. Cutler holds marathon length run-throughs of the show on Saturdays and Sundays, so during the week, I'm stuck calculating functions and pretending not to notice Andy ignoring me.

At Dom's special request, I even do my famous Andy countdown when Mrs. McCaffrey hands out the county championship practice sheets. The rest of the team joins in, but nothing distracts Andy from calculus. He doesn't even crack a smile, just blows through his work and sets down his pencil before we get to one. Everyone bursts into cheers.

The darn *Fill It In* achievement list is the only reason I refuse to bail on mathletes. Well, that, along with the fact that I can't stomach the thought of Andy chasing me away from something important. Because, for some reason, earning this varsity letter has become the ultimate achievement in my mind. Boring Sadie, who was happy to fly under the high school radar for the last three and half years, now has the potential to win the same award as a mathematical genius like Andrew Kosolowski. The Sadie Matthews whose previous award count totaled one—the nebulous senior superlative award, which is still surrounded by an air of mystery. I bet people think I'm like one of those super athletes later found out to be taking steroids. Everyone must suspect I rigged the

Most Likely to Get Married votes, but no one can pinpoint exactly how I did it. And, it's not like I even wanted that award. Who wants to have their future predicted for them? I want the excitement of figuring it out myself.

Plus, I promised Jana to do whatever it takes to make sure we fill in our entire list before graduation. Who would have thought adding and multiplying long columns of numbers would be my only shot for a stupid varsity letter? I sigh heavily and flip through my practice worksheets.

Back in January, I'd never have guessed how much winning a Senior Superlative Award and brainstorming a bunch of lame achievements would royally screw with my life.

Fill It In – April 2nd
Top Ten Ways to Cure Boredom
(When You're Stuck in the House Resting a Pulled Hamstring)

1. Re-watch every episode of The Vampire Diaries.
2. Write I Heart Andy over and over in the margins of your copybook.
3. Write Mrs. Sadie Kosolowski and then decide no matter how much you love your future husband, there is no way you are taking his name.
4. Word Finds. Lots of them.
5. Catch up on Fill It In because you've been too busy to work on your daily lists.
6. Paint your toenails black and then blue and then black again.
7. Practice origami with cheap napkins.
8. Memorize Jana's lines for Audrey II in case she completely freaks out on opening night.
9. Start thinking about college applications—just thinking, though.
10. Call Andy's cell phone (listed on the mathletes' roster) and hang up before he answers. Repeat fifty times.

Chapter Nineteen

Two weeks after my hamstring pull, Mom notices my slight but persistent limp. Without bothering to ask my opinion, she books me an after school appointment with Dr. Kosolowski.

"Mom. Please. Not Dr. K.," I say when she breaks the news to me on my way out the door.

"Why not? Do you want to see a female doctor now that you're, er, mature?" Her gaze drops to my chest, as if she's finally realizing I need to go bra shopping. Admittedly, I'm still on the small side, chest-wise, but I'd upgraded from a tank top five years ago. "If you have questions, I can ask for Adelaide, our nurse practitioner."

Not a medical question, I think. I just don't want to discuss his son. Or talk about waffles. Or how great the

Super K family is. The memory of the one meal I shared with Andy's family floats into my mind, and I feel as if an imaginary hand is tugging a shoestring looped around my heart. To avoid Mom's probing, I stick my head in the closet and root around for my spring jacket.

"Dr. Kosolowski is the best in town," she says, her voice muffled by the wool coat scratching the side of my face. "Plus, he knows you personally. In fact, last week he mentioned how you stopped by his house for breakfast one day. You're friends with his son? Andrew?"

Long pause. She's fishing. Let her sink her hook in someone else, because I am not going there.

"I'm late for school. Three-fifteen, right?" I locate my jacket, wrestle it off the hanger, and breeze out of the apartment.

"Three-fifteen. Have a good day, Sadie." She calls after me as I shuffle down the stairs, leaning on the railing to ease the pressure on my leg. She sounds heartbroken over my unwillingness to spill details. Since when is breakfast with Andy's family such big news? I sigh and hoist my back pack higher on my shoulder. Guilt is a powerful tool in Mom's arsenal.

***

Dr. Kosolowski's office always smells like extra-strength Lysol and rubbing alcohol. Stepping into the waiting room, I'm greeted by Day-Glo murals of monster-sized children painted on the walls. A mixture of hideous and cheery.

A motion sensor bings, informing Mom of my arrival. She glances up from the stack of files on her desk. Between patients, she works on updating the office's new computerized medical records system. Have I mentioned that my mother's computer skills rival her medical expertise? Thankfully, she's a people person.

"Busy day?" I ask when she slides the glass window open and hands me a sign-in sheet.

"You wouldn't believe," she says, tucking a stray lock of hair behind her ear. "Another stomach bug hit the preschool. Dr. Tim is in room three." In work, she refers to Andy's dad by his kid-friendly name. He strives to be both approachable and pronounceable for his young patients. Her desk phone rings and Mom slides the glass partition back into place.

I retrace my steps through the waiting room. Right as I reach the door to the examination area, it swings open and something large and solid barrels into me.

"Whoa," says Andy, backing up to keep from bulldozing over me. If "whoa" counts as a real word, it's the first time he's spoken to me in weeks.

"Sorry," I mutter, then, "Are you sick?" I eye him suspiciously. I can't risk catching anything contagious right now, especially a no holds barred, up-all-night stomach virus.

"No, I just stopped by to pick up some samples for my brother. His allergies kicked in, and my dad wants to switch his medication. The office is on the way home from school, so …" he trails off and looks away from me, seeming upset over his inability to ignore my existence.

"So you were being a good brother," I finish.

"Something like that. See you around." He steps around me, into the waiting room. "Bye, Ms. Matthews," I hear him call.

Suck up.

"Have a nice day, Andrew. Did you run into my daughter back there?"

"Yes, ma'am. Literally. I hope she feels better soon," Andy says. Sure he does. Cause it's no fun torturing weak-limbed, short people.

"Ah, there's Sadie." Dr. Kosolowski emerges from a room marked with his name in gold lettering and waves me deeper into the exam area. "Let's take a look at your leg. Your mother is worried."

He smiles broadly, as if we're sharing a secret joke. The memory of Dr. Tim frying up lumpy, fatty bacon in a nifty sweater vest flashes in my mind, and I cover my face with my hand to hide a nervous giggle. We crossed some sort of doctor/patient barrier over brunch. Did watching my participation in a waffle scarf-down change his opinion of me?

He steps into a dark room and I follow. A clicking noise precedes a flood of light. "Hand-activated switches harbor bacteria," he explains, as I blink at the brightness. "We use a no-touch system. Hop up on the table."

I attempt a hop, which turns into more of a backward plunk, setting off loads of crinkling paper action on top of the exam station. Dr. Kosowloski tests my reflexes with a mallet. Next, he contorts my knee in a variety of positions. He wraps up the exam by stretching out my leg.

"Hmm," he says, giving his professional opinion. "Walk for me." I slide off the table and limp in a small circle.

"Still bothering you, is it?"

"A bit. Not too bad, though."

"Level two hamstring pulls can take four to six weeks to heal. I believe exercising through pain isn't the best long-term solution for a young athlete like you. Is it imperative that you return to running this season?"

"Not at all," I say, doing a silent cheer and not bothering to correct his athlete label. "My non-athletic activities keep me busy."

"So I hear. Andy says you're quite an impressive mathlete."

Okay, that statement came out of left field.

"No one is as impressive as your son. He's fearsome when it comes to calculus."

"You must make a great team, then," Dr. Kosolowski responds, and I wonder if we're talking solely about math. "Let your competitors focus on the big guy while you sneak up from behind and crush them with your intellect."

He shadow boxes around the exam room for emphasis. Now, see, Dr. Tim has a sense of humor. What is his son's problem?

"I'll suggest your strategy to Mrs. McCaffrey." I lean away as his right hook nearly connects with my jaw. "Maybe we can take this mathletes thing all the way to states. Nationals."

"Phenomenal. Just don't overdo the victory parade on that leg of yours." And with that piece of friendly medical advice and a scribbled note to Coach Jenkins excusing me from the track team, I am sent packing.

***

As the end of April nears, tulips and daffodils push up from the ground, the sun rises before me on weekday mornings, and life settles into a new state of normal.

Ben and Jana become an official couple. They are disgustingly cute together.

Andy continues to treat me like a well-chewed piece of bubble gum clinging to the bottom of his extra-large high top.

According to the always-reliable *Out of Tune* gossip column, Dom and Giuliana are dating again. Their relationship appears to be a casual one. On his end, at least.

By the week before Spring Break, I am so ready for time off from play practice, math, and school in general. A full week without trigonometric functions. But, as luck would have it, at our final scheduled meet up before vacation, Mrs. McCaffrey announces our qualification for county competitions. To celebrate, she delivers a whole new binder of worksheets filled with problems for us.

Spring break homework. Super. And ninety-nine percent of the questions read as if written in a foreign language. But I'm willing to be a one per center if it gets me a varsity letter.

"Let's have a short session today. We can try a timed test," Mrs. McCaffrey suggests. "Who can solve the most equations in ten minutes?"

"Andy." The team shouts in unison. Our captain turns bright red, like a huge tomato with blond curls. Ignoring our response, Mrs. McCaffrey sets a timer on the smart board, and I begin checking off any problem I feel capable of at least attempting. I settle on line thirty, with only one x and one y to solve. Dom leans over and taps me on the shoulder.

"Hey, hot stuff."

When I turn toward him, the overpowering scent of his body spray accosts my nose. Nasty. Then, the thought crosses my mind that I no longer remember what Andy smelled like when we kissed, and I feel a dull pang of regret.

"Are you taking Giuliana to the prom?" I ask, hoping to distract him before he makes a huge scene at my expense.

"No clue. Why, do you need a date?" His right eyebrow rises, transforming his expression into something more sinister.

I scratch out the next step of my equation, pretending not to hear the question.

"I bet Mathman over there is free. Did he propose to you yet? Yo. AK." A wicked grin splits Dom's face. At the sound of his name, Andy looks up from his paper and levels his gaze at me. A hush falls over the room. Pencils pause as everyone takes time off from logic problems to tune into the latest episode of my Dom and Andy soap opera. Behind me, Jana snaps her bubble gum, warning me not to escalate the already tense situation.

"Shut up, Altomeri," Andy says, his voice low, but filled with daggers. Geez, Dominic hit a sore spot. Andy didn't even sound this mad when he found his name on the *Fill It In* list.

"Pi R squared to you too, buddy," Dominic shoots back. "Sadie, if you need a real man to take you to the prom, feel free to ask me, babe. I'm sure you can convince me to make myself available."

Jana digs her pencil in the center of my back, likely encouraging me to go along with Dom's suggestion. Doubling with her and Ben would be fun, but Dom's offer to make himself available is nowhere near the prom invitation of my dreams. A girl has to have some basic standards.

I shake my head and offer him a polite smile. "No, thanks, Dom. You should take your girlfriend. I'm sure she'd be disappointed if you went to the prom without her."

"Ah, she'll get over it." Dom shrugs and goes back to solving functions. In the front of the classroom, the smart board chirps.

"Okay, timed test is over. Hand in your worksheets on

the way out. I'll check everyone's answers over vacation," Mrs. McCaffrey says.

"Sounds like you've got some wild spring break plans, Mrs. M.," Dom says.

"With a strawberry daiquiri in hand," she adds, her face twisting into smile. I scrape back my chair, rushing to extricate myself from this latest Dom/Andy disaster and pass Mrs. McCaffrey my nearly blank paper before high-tailing it out of the room. When Andy silently passes my locker, I duck and cover, pretending to search through the mess for a lost text book. The hallway lights blink off, leaving me alone in the dark. Jana is long past the days of waiting around for me. Not with Ben waiting for her.

"You know, I'm really proud of you, Sadie." Mrs. McCaffrey steps out of her classroom.

I slam my locker door closed. "Proud of me? Why?"

"Because I see the way most girls look at Dominic. If he'd offered to take anyone else in that room to the prom, they would have jumped at the chance. But, I think you see what's inside of him. You look beyond his physical—um—characteristics."

I have to smile at Mrs. McCaffrey's choice of words. I wonder how often the topic of cute high school guys comes up in the faculty lunch room.

"So, are you saying I did the right thing?"

Mrs. McCaffrey pats my shoulder. "Definitely. If you were to ask my opinion, I would recommend that you hold out for the best man. I'm sure it's only a matter of time."

"I hope you're right, Mrs. McCaffrey. The prom is only a month away, and I have no idea how I'm going to find a date."

But actually, I'm starting to realize that I do.

Fill It In – April 20th
Top Ten Ways to Snag a Prom Date

1. Call 1-800-Prom-Date. (What? That's not a thing?)
2. Tape a list of the Top 10 Reasons to Go to Prom with Sadie on his locker. Because I rock at list writing.
3. Stand outside of his house with a poster.
4. Write on his windshield with that cool car paint.
5. Ask your best friend to ask him for you because you're a huge chicken.
6. Be poetic. Roses are Red, Violets are Blue, Let's Go to Prom and Get Married, Too.
7. Hijack the school's intercom system and make a public request during morning announcements.
8. Math Equation. You + Sadie = Best Prom Ever.
9. Ask Jana how to say "please go to the prom with me" in Spanish. That way, if he rejects me, only a limited number of people will understand.
10. Text Bombardment.

Chapter Twenty

"I need your help with a PPD," I say when Jana calls later that night.

"PPD? Blech. Sounds gross."

"Potential Prom Date, Jana. I have someone in mind."

"Thank Goodness, chica, 'cause you're running out of time."

"Yeah, and I have one tiny problem. He doesn't like me anymore."

"Are you talking about Andy?" she asks. "He so likes you."

"No, Jana. He has quite clearly said that he does *not* like me. Multiple times." I speak slowly into the phone to emphasize the seriousness of my predicament.

"What Andy says and what he means are two completely different things. He says he hates you because he feels used. And he's embarrassed because he liked kissing you, but he thinks you just did it for some stupid list."

"I did do it for the list. But I didn't hate kissing him."

"Then why didn't you tell him the truth?"

I sigh. "Because everything with Andy seems momentous. He would expect something. And after that ridiculous Super Superlative vote, I feel like everyone expects something. It's too much pressure. Why can't kissing someone be fun?"

"Kissing someone and marrying them are two very different things. Kissing Ben is lots of fun." I hear the smile in Jana's voice.

"I know, I know. And by the time I realized I wanted something with Andy, he hated me. Now when I see him, he's griping about how I used him for a list or dropping me on my ass after I ripped apart my hamstring."

"You know, if Andy didn't care so much, he wouldn't complain so much. He would have laughed about the double snogging the way Dominic did."

Jana's observation sends me bounding off my bed and circling around the apartment in a state of extreme excitement. "You are so right. Finally, something makes sense!"

"And there's the light bulb."

"I need to fix this. Operation 'Get Sadie A Prom Date' is on."

Jana laughs softly through the phone. "Poor Andy. He doesn't have a chance, does he?"

"Nope. He picked the wrong girl to pretend to hate but secretly like."

***

The next morning I intercept Jana at her locker before Ben gets to her. Colette is present as well, a big smile on her face, happy to be included in any conversation revolving around Andy.

"Do we have a plan?" Jana asks, anxious to move on and spend a few minutes with Ben before homeroom.

I frown. "Not really. Spring break is next week, and I don't even know if Andy's going out of town. Should we just wait until after?"

Jana swats my arm. "No way. You cannot lose almost two weeks. The prom vultures are circling your man."

My stomach turns at the thought of losing Andy to a junior or sophomore who's simply using him for a chance to attend the senior prom. "What should I do? He won't talk to me."

"He'll talk to me," Colette offers in her mini-mouse voice. "Why don't I ask him if he has plans for next week? At least you'll know that much."

"Would you, Colette?" I ask.

"Sure, but I'll need something in return."

"Little sister, you drive a hard bargain," Jana says.

"What do you want?" I ask, my shoulders sagging. Paybacks with Colette are never fun.

"Friday night at Starbucks. I want to hang out with you and Jana."

"Sorry. I have a date," Jana says.

"Fine." Colette pokes my arm. "Just you."

We seal the deal with a handshake. In exchange for one brief conversation with Andy, I promise to make an appearance with her at the Main Street Starbucks. Friday night with a bunch of giggly freshman girls. I must be sick in the head.

The three of us agree to run a stake out at Andy's locker Friday morning. When he appears at the far end of the hallway, Colette moves in for the kill. But someone else gets to Andy first.

"Can I talk to you for a second? I need your help." Andy's progression down the hallway is interrupted by Melinda Banner. She approaches from the opposite direction, her deep red hair braided into a long rope, swishing side to side. She hands him a written request for tutoring signed by Mrs. McCaffrey. Andy squints at the paper as if he's forgotten to how to read. Eventually he speaks to Melinda, briefly working out a meeting time and place.

Melinda's expression turns nothing short of smarmy as she waves to Jana and me, and then nearly plows into Colette, who by this time has planted herself next to Andy's locker.

Jana spies her lab partner Arlene across the hall, so we drift in her direction, pretending to be fascinated with the photo collage taped inside her locker door.

"So, Andy, are you packing for spring break?" Colette asks in her squeaky voice, following the script I emailed to her last night. The target, as Jana now refers to Andy, looks up and down, around and behind him, obviously confused. This must be the first time Jana's little sister found the nerve to ask him a personal question.

"Uh, hey, Colette. Actually, I'm staying in town next week. I picked up some extra flight time."

"Oh. Cool," she says and giggles nervously. Then, Colette stuns those of us pretending not to listen to the conversation by deviating from my instructions and asking a follow-up question. "Andy, would you be my date for the freshman dance?" Her cute little chipmunk cheeks stain bright red, like two apples jettisoning from the rest of her face.

"What!" I hiss into Jana's ear. "How dare she take

advantage of my bribery?"

"Just as friends," Jana whispers, placing her hand on my arm. "Colette knows how you feel. She's—"

"And here's a shot of me after I took off my shirt," Arlene announces. "We were protesting the fashion industry's inhumane treatment of animals."

Jana leans forward, examining the blurry photo. "Isn't that just a cotton T-shirt in your hand?"

"Uh, yeah, but we wanted to use nudity to make our point."

I glance across the hallway when Arlene points out additional topless images I know for sure will be forever branded in my mind if I dare look at them. Twenty years from now, I want to remember the fully dressed Arlene.

Meanwhile, Andy appears taken aback by Colette's request. "Uh, sure. When is it again?"

I bite my lip to keep from laughing at the way he flounders through a less than enthusiastic acceptance.

After the freshman dance details are hammered out, Colette risks a glance my way. I force a smile for her benefit. If young and big-brained is Andy's type, I'll never be able to compete, anyway.

***

"Where does Andy hang out in his free time?" I ask Jana as we wait in line at Starbucks on the first day of spring break, which we've dubbed as Mocha Latte Monday. Our short-term goals for the week include sleeping past nine a.m. and consuming as many caffeinated beverages as possible.

"Besides the corner of Main and State after snow storms?" Jana responds, sweeping her eyes through the student-heavy crowd. "No idea. Why not take a direct approach and call him?"

I mentally scoff at her suggestion. "Like he would answer my call."

"If he refuses to talk to you, then stand outside his house with an 'I love you, Andy' sign."

I shake my head. "Too lunatic."

"How about taking a walk around the playground? He has that herd of younger siblings to deal with."

"Absolutely not. Even if he does the big brother thing and takes the kids out somewhere, I can't flirt in front of an audience."

We file inside the steamy coffee house, order our drinks and carry them out. Caffeine-addicted teenagers spill out onto the street, willing to block traffic rather than lose their place in line. Balancing my hot cup in one hand, I boost myself over the legs of a couple sophomores sitting on the curb. This year, our late April weather feels more Toronto-like than Miamish. Gusty wind flaps a paper taped to a light post on the corner.

"Oh, look, free food at the Airport Open House. And hot rock band guys playing," Jana says, pointing to the flyer.

"Andy takes flying lessons at the airport," I mention, striving for nonchalance.

"Jackpot!" Jana motions pulling the arm of a slot machine. "He'll definitely be there, chica."

"What does one wear to an airport open house?"

"Maybe one of those Snoopy Red Baron flying hats with the goggles?"

"Or a mini skirt stewardess outfit from the sixties?"

Jana's eyes light up. "Even better. We have five days to find you a perfect outfit."

***

To keep my mind off my boy problems, I soak up the break week babysitting a bunch of grade school kids whose parents either couldn't take off from work, or more likely didn't want to waste precious vacation time when their kids are home from school. I also offer to walk every dog in my apartment complex to boost my prom dress savings. Just in case I find a date and need to shop.

Jana stops by my apartment while Ben runs ten miles in the mornings. She gave up on track shortly after Andy's father wrote my medical excuse note. By the time Saturday rolls around, we've spent hours going through our clothes, searching for an appropriate outfit. With Jana's approval, I settle on a new pair of jeggings, purchased with a chunk of my spring break earnings, and a sky blue Abercrombie tee.

After she leaves, I discover a leather bomber jacket in the back of the coat closet.

The jacket looks and smells manly, like gasoline and old leather. I have no idea where it came from, but the size is way too big for my mother. Weird. Mom never brings guys home. And I would know if one of my few and far between dates left an article of clothing behind.

***

"Cool jacket," Jana approves when she and Ben swing by to pick me up late Saturday afternoon.

"This old thing? I found it in the closet, calling my name."

"I'll bet it was," Jana says, poking me with her elbow. "Waiting for a special occasion, right?"

Downstairs, Ben's minivan chariot awaits. With my permission, Jana updates him on my catch a prom date plan, not because I want him to know how desperate I am to nab Andy, but because I assume everything I tell her is brought up in later conversation anyway. At least Ben is a trustworthy guy. Plus, Jana threatens to dump him if he blabs our secrets to anyone, even Dominic. Especially Dominic.

One mile before the airport, we hit a roadblock on Skyline Avenue. We ditch the van in a nearby field and sift through high grass, cutting our own path toward the jam-packed open house. Every infant, toddler, tween and pre-teen in Harmony must have decided they want to be pilots when they grow up.

"Where's the boy band?" Jana asks, scanning the crowd for hot guys with guitars. Ben points to a raised platform ten yards behind the cracked, asphalt runway where five wrinkly guys with long, grey hair play banjos.

"What happened to the rock stars?" I ask. Around us, meltdowns and tantrums drown out the roar of jet engines. The mob hanging around a ring toss game incites a near riot when a bunch of big kids try to budge their way in the front of the line.

"This is really how you girls want to spend the afternoon?" Ben stops in his tracks and sniffs twice. "Hey, I smell funnel cake."

"Do not bring it near me!" Jana sucks in a horrified breath. "My prom dress was just altered." She brushes her lips over Ben's cheek and then whispers something in his ear. Ben's face burns red. His mouth drops open. Without a word of good-bye, he walks off.

"What was that about?" I ask.

"I described my dress for him. He needs a second," Jana says, gazing after Ben's retreating form with a smug expression.

"Sadie!" Andy's little sister breaks apart from a crowd of elementary schoolers and tugs on the sleeve of my jacket. Her two front teeth have grown in and they're only slightly crooked. My heart skips a beat when I realize her brother must be close.

"Hi …" I completely blank on her name. Probably not Andyette, which is how I always think of her.

"Abby," she says, very helpfully. Close enough to Andy that I won't forget it again.

"Hi, Abby." I bend my knees, crouching down to her size. "This is my friend Jana. Jana, this is Andy's sister."

"Hi, Abby," Jana says and then, "Is your brother here?"

"Andy's flying the plane." One of Abby's pigtails brushes my face when she turns to point at the sky above the runway. "He's landing now. Wanna go see?"

A small plane drones overhead, beginning its descent.

When the left wing tilts at a steep angle, I nearly bite through my lower lip. My future prom date is going to crash! After what seems like light years, but is probably less than ten seconds, the plane straightens out again, drops on the runway, bounces twice, and finally settles on the ground. The brakes screech and bright orange sparks fly out from under the wheels.

"Oh, Abby, there you are. Don't walk away from me, sweetie. You'll get lost in the crowd." Mrs. Kosolowski appears, holding her hand above her eyes to shield the bright sun as she watches Andy's plane taxi closer.

"But I wasn't lost," Abby insists. "I was with Sadie. And her friend Jana."

"Hello, girls. Did you see Andrew's landing? He's gotten much better." Mrs. Kosolowski greets us with a warm smile.

"You call that a good landing?" My voice ranges an octave higher than normal. "I was sure he was going to crash! How do you let him do that?"

Mrs. K. smiles and pats my arm soothingly. "Andrew is very conscientious. He took it upon himself to thoroughly research the probability of student pilot accidents before asking for lessons."

"Sounds like the Andy we all know and love," Jana says.

Mrs. K. continues rubbing my arm, like she can hear

my heart pounding. "I will admit, the thought of him controlling an airplane sometimes keeps me up at night. We've missed you at breakfast, Sadie. The little ones keep asking Andrew when you're coming back. Apparently, your waffles taste even better than mine."

Over Mrs. Kosolowski's shoulder, I catch Jana's look of surprise. She realizes I held back valuable Andy information.

"Um, well, I've been busy. With the school play, and mathletes, and everything." And because my invitation was mostly likely revoked when Andy found out about me kissing Dominic.

"Well, you're always welcome. Don't wait for my son to invite you. Are you here to watch him fly?"

"Yes, in fact, that's exactly why I'm here," I say.

"Come with me, then. I'm on my way to check in with him." Mrs. Kosolowski links her arm through mine, refusing to take no for an answer. Abby tags along behind us, chattering about waffles, her annoying older brothers, and my cool jacket. I glance back in Jana's direction for help, but she's already taken off in the opposite direction, on the hunt for Ben.

When I turn my attention back to the airplane, I spot Andy unlatching the door and springing onto the runway. A swarm of young kids presses forward, shouting questions about flying. Behind Andy's fan club stands a group of freshman and sophomore girls, including Colette, whose smile stretches from her left ear to her right.

Nerdy Andy has groupies. My eyes remain glued on him, wishing he would just notice me. But my hopes are dashed when a tall, auburn-haired girl steps out of the crowd and gives Andy a fierce hug. Melinda Banner. What's she doing here? Is this really the best time for math tutelage? She doesn't have a backpack with her or anything.

Colette's mini-obsession with Andy doesn't worry me too much. But Melinda scares me. Why does she want Andy? She ranks much higher than me on the popularity chain and probably could have just about any guy she wanted. Yes, Andy's cute and he's older and more mature and probably going to be as rich as Mark Zuckerberg one day. And the flying ace persona definitely increases his coolness factor. Okay, I think I just answered my own question.

My heart sinks in my chest, yet I stand there, frozen, beside Andy's mom, forcing myself to remain stoic.

"Oh my," says Mrs. K, taking in the flock of Andy admirers.

"I guess everyone loves a pilot." I inject false cheerfulness into my voice. "I think I'll catch up with Andy later. Tell him I said congratulations on the safe landing."

I skirt away, easily blending in with the throngs of mini-humans, struggling to hold back the tears stinging my eyes. My mind feels like it's filled with clumps of fuzzy cotton. It's not until I bump into the huge person obstructing my path that I realize I've wandered into a display of antique cars parked by the control tower.

Two strong hands grab my upper arms, steadying me. "Everything okay, Miz Matthews?"

I knew I'd eventually run into Mr. Drum again, but did it have to be now?

I brush the leather sleeve of my jacket over my face to soak up my tears. "Fine, Mr. Drum. Sorry, I didn't see you there."

Amusement flashes in his camo-green eyes. "Usually, I'm hard to miss."

"Right. I must have been caught up in the beauty of all these ... cars."

"Fine pieces of machinery," he agrees.

At this point, the conversation stalls because I have absolutely nothing further to contribute. I can't even make eye contact with him, due to potential fatal humiliation.

"Nice jacket," Mr. Drum steps back and inspects my costume.

"Thanks. I'll see you around. In school, I guess," I say and walk off, still in a fog.

I text Jana to tell her I'm near the antique automobiles

and lower myself onto an empty bench to wait for her. Shoving my hands into the pockets of my jacket, I pull out a button, a crumpled up slip of paper, and a business card for Nat's Tats. When I unfold the paper, I see my mom's cell phone number written in her jumbled cursive. Given my mom's penchant for construction workers, the tattoo card isn't a total surprise. Could she be secretly dating someone? Why wouldn't she tell me about him if she was? Geez-us, I hope he's not a total loser.

"How'd it go with Andy?" Jana's voice shakes me out of my stupor. She plops down on the bench beside me.

"Terrible," I say, suddenly remembering why I'm even here at the airport. "I didn't talk to him. He's a star pilot now, and every girl in Harmony loves him. Melinda Banner was his personal greeter when he stepped off the plane."

"Melinda? I though he was just tutoring her."

"They looked like they have a very friendly tutoring relationship. Maybe she's interviewing him about his availability for the prom."

"Ha, Andy's so dense he'd probably wind up with her as a date without even realizing it."

"For someone so smart he sure acts dumb around girls. And your sister was front and center at the worship service."

"Colette's here? The stinker, she must have overheard

us talking. So, what, you just walked away without fighting for your prom date of destiny?"

When I don't answer, Jana picks up the half-filled tub of caramel corn resting on her lap and offers it to me. I must really be out of it if I missed the scent of melted caramel.

"Ben isn't helping with my prom diet. He keeps buying junk food," she says, munching away. "He has calories to burn. But, I'm not running ten miles a day anytime soon."

Silently, I pass her the business card and reach in the tub. While she reads, I ingest the sticky mixture of salty and sweet, popped to perfection.

"A tattoo parlor? Are you going to ink Andy's initials on your butt?"

"No! The card and my Mom's cell phone number were in the pocket of my jacket. The one left in the coat closet at my apartment."

"Wow. Your Mom is tight with Nat, the premier ink artist in the tristate area?" Jana squints at the card as she recites the faded words.

"If she is, she hasn't ever mentioned him."

"Is she dating a heavily tattooed person?"

"Not that I know of. Maybe she's thinking of ditching her medical receptionist career and starting a new business?"

"Maybe," Jana says, her eyes sweeping over the miles of leather I'm wearing.

"What? It's possible."

"Sure it is," Jana says. "So, you're not gonna obsess over this little mystery, are you?"

"Not at all," I promise. Beneath the overlong sleeves of my jacket, my fingers are crossed.

Chapter Twenty-One

For the rest of the weekend, I do everything but pitch a tent, light a campfire, and roast marshmallows in my room to avoid my mother. Granted, she's probably confused by my sudden transformation into a typical sulky teenager, but she's also smart enough not to push me into a confrontation.

For once, I'm entitled to some full-fledged angst. I have reasons. First, after years of going unnoticed by most of the female population of Harmony, Andy has morphed into a local celebrity. I've finally realize we're meant to be together at the same time he starts attracting girls like he's Capitan America or something.

And what is Mom hiding? She never talks much

about her personal life, but I'd always thought that was because she didn't have one. Could Nat from Nat's Tats be the answer to my question?

My late night call wakes Jana up.

"I need to talk to Nat," I tell her.

"Nat who?" she murmurs into the phone, her voice slurred by sleep.

"The tattoo guy. Nat's Tats. Maybe the jacket belongs to one of his customers. You know, a first-timer who wanted my mom's initials on his bicep. Something tasteful."

"Oh, Nat," Jana says, suddenly alert. "Can we talk about this tomorrow?"

"I'm going to Nat's. Tonight. He's open seven days a week until midnight. Or, at least that's what this business card says."

"You shouldn't go to a tattoo parlor alone," she mumbles, yawning big.

"Right. You're absolutely right. See you tomorrow."

"Sadie, don't—"

I press the end call button on my phone.

***

For the first time ever, I sneak out of my apartment. Mom isn't home, anyway. Sunday is Bon Jovi night at The Green Lagoon Pub. Now that I think about it, she hasn't been home much at all lately, but I'd been too busy myself to notice. I switch on the side lamp in my room and close the door, hoping she'll think I'm studying.

My stroll through downtown Harmony takes less than twenty minutes. Even in the emptiness of night, I feel the calm embrace of my hometown. Along the side streets, I recognize the names on most of the mailboxes.

Nat's Tats is located on the first floor of a rickety old house crammed between a bunch of questionable-looking businesses. A red neon sign flashes "Open" in the dark window. Good to know Nat keeps to his publicized hours.

Inside, the sound of snake charmer music floating in from another room greets me. A bell sits on the counter, and my fingers hover, about to hit the ringer, when a loud voice says, "Don't even think about it."

I drop my hand and jump back from the counter. Along the back wall, crushed red velvet curtains part, exposing a doorway to another darkened room. If I don't die tonight, Jana will kill me when I tell her about coming here alone.

A guy who looks like the Incredible Hulk, minus the green skin, smashes through the gap in the curtains. My mathlete instincts kick in, and I find myself estimating the circumference of his upper arms and comparing them to tree trunks. Possibly something in the giant oak or redwood family.

"Need something, kid?" he grumbles. Geez, do I look that young? I should have worn my high heeled boots.

"Is Nat here?" I ask, my voice sounding squeaky, like Colette's.

"Yo, NAT!" The force of his voice shakes the black and white images of inked body parts hanging on the wall.

"WHAAAAT?" replies a strange voice. Strange, because it's not what I expected to hear.

A huge woman rolls through the curtains. Seriously. Like Bertha the amazing land-whale.

"Another underager?" Beady eyes peer out from mountains of tattoo-covered flesh. "Ya got parental permission?"

"Are you—are you Nat?" I stammer, thinking I've found the perfect Audrey II.

"Yeah. Who are you?"

"Sadie Matthews. I found your card in my mom's jacket, and I thought you might be her ... friend." Not exactly Mom's jacket, but it was in our apartment, so close enough.

"Are you Kathleen Matthews' daughter?"

"Yes, I am." Apparently, Mom's famous in the tattoo circuit.

Nat roars. "Gah! Didn't know she had a daughter. But ya look just like her."

"When was the last time you saw my mom?"

"I see her around. Green Lagoon sometimes. She never comes here for tats, but she used to hang out in the shop once in a while. Then she went all legit and got a real job. Too highbrow for the tattoo parlor, that snooty pants." Nat—actually Natalie, I guess, busts out in a chest-cracking laugh. I smile. Mom and I are not highbrow by any stretch of one's imagination.

"So, what do you want? A swan? Princess tiara? That's what most of the young girls ask for."

"Oh, no. Mom would kill me," I rush to say. "I just found your card, and wondered …"

"If your ma's hiding a tattoo?" Nat breaks into a grin, revealing a mouth three teeth short of being full. "Naw, she's a preppie. Totally gag me with a spoon. That's what we used to say when we went to school together. Don't know what Scotty Drum sees in her."

***

Mom and Mr. Drum? My mom, who spent the last seventeen years warning me to stay away from dangerous boys, is dating the most supreme example of a bad boy all grown up.

After Nat's stunning revelation, sleep is no longer part of my nighttime agenda. I lay in bed, wide awake, waiting for a Monday morning that cannot come fast enough. Slipping into the leather jacket, I set off for school at an ungodly early hour, intending to stop by and see Mr. Drum before I completely lose my nerve.

After surviving the torture of Driver's Ed, descending into the depths of the basement auto shop feels like reentering the gates of hell. Only the distant whine of a drill disrupts the tomb-like silence. When no one answers my knock, I enter the shop and nearly barge into Mr. Drum, who reached the door the same time I did.

"Miz Matthews, can I help you with something?" He steps away and grabs a greasy towel dangling from the lecture podium to wipe off his hands. The scent of motor oil burns inside my nostrils. My clothes are gonna reek for the rest of the day.

"Um," I say, sounding completely brain dead. My stomach clenches hard to prevent a Greek yogurt uprising. "How are you today, Mr. Drum?"

He looks me up and down, once again taking in the sight of my leather jacket. "I'm alive. It's better than the alternative," he answers.

"Why, are you dying?" I ask, horrified. Just Mom's luck.

"No. Not as far as I know." He laughs a deep, gravelly laugh, picks up his drill, and pokes a large metal spike into the end. "Hey, didn't I give you an A in Driver's Ed?"

"Yes. Um, thank you for that."

He shrugs his enormous shoulders. "Don't thank me. It wasn't a gift. I would have given you an A-plus if you had come up with a better list of driving distractions." Thankfully, his face is buried in the engine of a car as he says this.

"About that ..." I start to say, but Mr. Drum holds up one hand to stop me.

"Did you have a driving question or are you here to sign up for another class? Just for the fun of it?"

"No. No more classes," I rush to say. "But I thought we might–I wanted to ask ..." I can't do it. Cannot summon the courage to ask him the most personal of personal questions.

So, I swallow hard and back up until the door knob presses into the small of my back. "Sorry, Mr. Drum. I have to go."

He gives a low whistle. "Nice jacket, Miz Matthews. I had one just like it, but I seem to have misplaced it."

Information overload! An alarm blares in my head and

the world tips sideways. I maneuver around the pesky door knob and out of the auto shop. When I glance back to make sure Mr. Drum hasn't followed me, I bash up against Andy and Sidh, on their way to the lower level computer lab.

"You okay, Sadie?" Sidh asks, latching onto my arm to prevent me from hitting the floor. "You look kind of– green." Andy is silent, but I notice his head bobbing back and forth between me and the open auto shop door.

"I'm fine. Gotta go. I'm late for—I'm just late."

***

Over lunch, I update Jana on my conversation with Mr. Drum. A better description might be lack of conversation, accompanied by rude gawking, but I keep that part to myself.

"He's so dating your Mom," Jana says. "He recognized the jacket. I knew it couldn't be the tattoo guy."

I munch on a carrot stick to avoid explaining Nat's inability to be my mother's guy.

"I can't believe my mom attracted such a—hunk, for lack of a better word." I shake my head.

"I can think of better words to describe Mr. Drum,

but given this morning's events we can't use them without sounding perverted. Who would have guessed that our Driver's Ed teacher is shacking up with your mother?"

"Do you think he'll give me free driving lessons?"

"Mr. Drum understands your driving potential better than anyone else on the planet. I bet he never gets into a car with you behind the wheel."

"You know what? I'll take that bet. We can add it to our list of achievements. Sadie gets Mr. Drum to teach her how to drive."

"Seriously? You think he would be able to just sit there and watch you run a stop sign?"

"This may sound crazy, but I do. It's funny how I sat in his class for months and it never struck me that we had a connection."

"No offense, Sadie, but picturing your mom and Mr. Drum in a romantic situation is just plain weird."

"Totally. Maybe the tattoos threw me off, but I always thought that if my mom met the love of her life, he would be some wrinkly, old guy who wears sweater vests and works in an office."

"And birds would sing, and the three of you would instantly be a happy step-family."

"I guess no one gets a fairy tale. And now I have to ask my mom if she's hot for my teacher."

"Later. Forget about your mom's love life until you

sort out your own dating catastophe. I passed Andy in the hallway before lunch, and Melinda Banner was all over him. Again."

I glance at the senior boys' lunch table and sure enough, Melinda's talking to Andy, shaking her perfect long hair over her shoulder, waves of auburn flowing down her back. She leans forward as she speaks, allowing him the opportunity to gaze longingly at her chest if he so desires. But clueless Andy aims his eyes at his text book, oblivious to her flirting.

Observing from a distance, I'm forced to admit Melinda and Andy make a perfect couple. In addition to her popularity credentials, she's decently smart, although she's apparently met her match in pre-Calculus.

"They're probably just comparing calculators," Jana says, following my gaze.

"Yeah, and with her bosoms blocking his view of the rest of the world, he'll never notice me. I don't know why I thought I had a chance with him. He barely talks to me anymore—all because I kissed someone else."

"Wouldn't you be mad, if it happened to you?" Jana asks, a bit too rationally. "If Andy kissed another girl and then kissed you—at the same party?"

"Snogging two boys at the same party was never my idea of fun. I was trying to be wild. Different. Someone I'm not."

"Andy likes who you are, not who you were trying to be."

I sigh and press the heel of my hand into my forehead. "Crazy isn't it?"

"Totally. After twelve years—"

"Eleven and a half—"

"Right. Chica, I'm sorry. I would never have encouraged you to kiss him if I knew you two really liked each other. But you always complained about him. And he acts dorky around every girl. I didn't realize he was being an extra big moron especially for you!" Jana waves her hands in the air as she rants, the way she always does when she get really worked up about a particular topic.

"I know. I totally get it. I have no one to blame but myself." I sigh and dunk my spoon into a fruit cup. "Do you think if I apologize to him, he'll like me again? Maybe ask me to the prom?"

"If you apologize to him, and truly mean it, I guarantee he will forgive you. But will you get a prom date out of it?" Jana shakes her head and gives me a sad smile. "I'm not sure. Andy's shooting up the Harmony High datable guy charts these days."

***

Resolving to make one final attempt with Andy, I wait by his locker after school, but he's nowhere in sight. After running down a mental list of his usual haunts, I check Mrs. McCaffrey's room, even though mathletes are off today.

"Looking for someone, Sadie?" Mrs. McCaffrey pushes aside the stack of papers she's grading when I poke my head in the classroom.

"Sorry, Mrs. McCaffrey. I thought I might find, um, Jana, in here," I lie.

"Oh. Because I was going to say, if you're looking for Andy, I saw him walking into the library."

Of course he was. Harmony High geek paradise.

"I wasn't looking for Andy," I insist, weakly.

"No problem. I believe you. But, if you wanted to accidentally run in to him, I would check the study area on the second floor. He might be tutoring this afternoon."

"Thanks, Mrs. McCaffrey."

"I'm rooting for you, Sadie," she says before shooing me out the door.

Sure enough, I find Andy squirreled away with Melinda Banner in a deserted area of the study section, their heads bent so close their foreheads almost touch. Hiding behind the bookshelves, I hear the breathy waves of Melinda's laughter, followed by Andy's deep, Muppety heh-heh.

I roam around the study area until I happen to pass by their table, for about the fifth time. When Andy manages to tear his eyes from his study partner, he looks like he wishes I would just disappear.

"Hi, guys," I say, forcing a friendly smile.

"Hey, Sadie," Melinda answers in an annoyed voice. Andy tilts his head in my direction.

"Andy, do you have a minute? I need to talk to you about our group project."

"What group project?" He stares me down from behind a new pair of slick black frames.

"You know, the one we're working on. As a group." I lift my chin, refusing to kiss his ass in front of an underclasswoman.

Andy tosses his pencil on to the study table and huffs loudly. Melinda shoots me a killer glare when he raises his long body out of a miniscule plastic chair. I lead him to the closest aisle of bookshelves, and just like that we're lost in the depths of nonfiction. Obviously, not a popular library area, because the air is thick with dust and the books look like they've morphed together after decades of abandonment. Behind Andy's head, I spy biographies of famous people whose last names begin with K. Don King. Larry King. Martin Luther King. Stephen King.

I inhale a deep breath and try to refocus.

"What's up?" Andy asks, with the same tone of

annoyance he's directed at me every time we've spoken since he read my list of apparently not so awesome achievements.

"I wanted to apologize about what happened at Dom's party."

"Why?"

"Why what?"

"Why do you care?"

"Um, because you thought I was just using you for my list?"

A muscle jumps in his cheek. "So it's true, then. You kissed me because of some stupid list you and Jana made up?"

"Well, it's kind of a funny story." I manage a shaky laugh. Andy's expression remains rockish. "Um, Jana thought I should kiss you because if we didn't seize the moment, we might not have another shot at that particular accomplishment. I didn't think it was a good idea, but I agreed to try. And then, the situation didn't work out exactly the way I thought it would." I raise my hands, surrendering to the anger he's about to direct at me.

"You kissed me twice."

"Come again?" I ask, directing my eyes away from a decrepit-looking Billie Jean King autobiography.

"Why did you kiss me twice?" he asks in a low voice,

leaning closer. Survival instinct kicks in and I flinch back, slamming into the shelves behind me. My shoulder blades scrape the wall of books, and I yelp.

"The way I read your list, you wanted to kiss two different guys, but only one kiss per guy, correct?" he continues, ignoring my pain. "Or did I misinterpret something?"

"No. I mean, no, you didn't misinterpret anything. I kissed you twice because I kind of, um, liked doing it."

Behind the black frames, his blue eyes squeeze shut. "Did you kiss Dumbchuk twice?"

"Geez-us, you should be a lawyer, you know that?" I smack myself in the forehead. "Who is Carole King?"

"What?" He glances side to side, confused.

"Nothing. Sorry. No, Andy, to answer your question, I did not kiss Dominic twice. Once was way more than enough."

A heh-heh rises from Andy's chest. He bows his shoulders, straining for self-control. I interpret this as a positive sign.

Resting his chin in his hand, he ponders my answer. "One kiss could be viewed as a simple anomaly."

"Okay, sure. Whatever." Like I know what an anomaly is. Standing this close to him for the first time in weeks, my brain isn't equipped to process fourth grade vocabulary, let alone Andy-speak. "So, can we be friends again?"

"Yes. Friends." He offers me his hand.

"Good. Great. I'll let you get back to your study date," I say, keeping my fingers wrapped around his.

"Not a date," he rushes to correct me. "Melinda has a test tomorrow and she's hit some sort of mental block with the theorems."

Sure she has. "Oh, right. Enjoy that then." I release my hold on him and turn to go. As I stroll down the K aisle, I need to physically hold back from kicking up my heels.

I kissed Andy twice.

He isn't dating Melinda.

My prom dream is alive.

Fill It In – Random List
10 Reasons Why I Still Might Nab the Prom Date of My Dreams

1. He smiled at me in homeroom. A real, happy Andy smile.
2. He isn't dating Melinda, even though she's a hotter, younger chick.
3. I kissed him twice. Plus, the anomaly thing.
4. Andy initiated the second kiss, so he must have enjoyed the first one.
5. We've known each other forever, so it would be nice to celebrate the end of twelve years of side-by-side learning at the senior prom. Together. With more kissing.
6. His Mom likes me. At least she used to like me. I hope he didn't tell her about the party at Dominic's house.
7. I caught him checking me out in mathletes after he finished the competition problems ten minutes before everyone else. He was probably just bored.
8. Then I overheard him tell Sidh that he hasn't asked anyone to the prom yet. He must be holding out for the best woman.

9. I know he's the best man. So I'm holding out for him. Even though I haven't had any offers besides Dumbchuck.

10. Good karma surrounds me. Jana said the moon's over Jupiter, which is a positive sign in her world. It's got to happen. Soon, I hope.

Chapter Twenty-Two

After making progress with Andy, I decide the time has come to confront my mother. To soften her up, I whip up her favorite dinner–egg white omelets. I spend a full hour chopping vegetables and shredding a block of yellow cheddar cheese, after slicing off the moldy corners.

"What smells so good?" Mom asks when she pushes in the door after work.

"My culinary masterpiece," I reply, mimicking Mrs. Rodriguez's French accent.

"Did you get detention again?" Mom drops her suitcase-sized purse on the sofa and stands, hands on hips, eyes narrowed.

"No, nothing like that."

"Do you need money?"

"No, Mom. I wanted to have a nice dinner. Just the two of us, like it's always been. As a family." Emphasis on family. And potential ex-Army Rangers who may join our family dynamic at some point in the future. In particular, ex-Army Rangers who also teach at Harmony High School.

Mom kicks off her platforms with a sigh and pads her way into the dining area. I set a plate of eggs and veggies in front of her and then detour into the coat closet. When I return, the leather jacket is draped over my shoulders.

"Does this belong to you?"

A sliver of egg white slides from her fork. "Where did you find that?"

"In the coat closet."

Mom takes a long sip of orange juice.

"Grandpop's not the bomber jacket type," I continue.

"Not unless it matches his polyester pants," she says, with a snort. "Put it away."

The toaster dings and two slices of bread launch skyward before falling onto the counter. Mom shoves her chair back and disappears into the kitchen to retrieve them.

"It's Mr. Drum's jacket, isn't it?" I follow her, relentless now.

She takes a bite of toast and chokes on the dry bread.

After a round of coughing, she says, "That's pulling a name out of thin air. Mr. Drum, your Driver's Ed teacher?"

"Yeah. The one who's ripped and has awesome thick, dark hair. Why didn't you tell me?"

She heaves a sigh and finally, finally turns to face me. "What was I supposed to say? Oh, by the way, Sadie, I've been dating your Driver's Ed instructor for the last five months."

"Five months!" I scream.

She laughs nervously. "About that."

"Did you even think *he* might say something to me?"

"He didn't know—not at first, anyway."

"Didn't know what? That you stole his jacket?"

"I didn't *steal* his jacket. He left it here the night you slept over Jana's."

"The night before my DRIVER'S ED EXAM?" I shriek. "The night before I made a complete ass of myself in front of him?"

"What did you do now?" Fear flickers in Mom's eyes.

"Uh, nothing. Never mind. What didn't he know?"

She casts her eyes away from me, and takes another, smaller bite of toast. "When we first met, he didn't know I had a kid. Then he got his class roster and saw your last name."

"Aha. He caught you in a lie."

She uses a knife to cut off a burnt crust, then sinks

back into her seat at the table, as if a calm, quiet dinner is still possible. Meanwhile, I'm catching flies with my gaping mouth. "So, what, you're not serious? This is just a casual ... thing?"

Mom snickers. "I might be serious. But I don't know what Scott is."

"And Scott," I struggle to release the name from my mouth, "doesn't want to get to know your daughter?"

"I don't know. Honestly, I don't know. At first there was just this burning physical attraction ..."

"MOM!" I cover my ears with my hands. "Stop. Skip ahead."

"Okay, you're right. Inappropriate. But he has such nice hair. And good teeth. And his biceps ... and the cleft chin."

"All fabulous. Go on."

"At first I didn't know how to tell him. But one day he asked me, point blank. I couldn't really deny you."

"Did you want to?"

"No. Of course not. Never."

"So now he knows."

"Yes, but I made him swear not to tell anyone that we were together. I didn't want people to think you took advantage of my personal relationship to pass his class."

"Oh, really? You've been sneaking around to protect me?"

"He only comes over when you're at Jana's." She catches my look of horror and her face crumples. "I wanted to tell you. But, he's so ..."

"Good looking?"

"Okay, yes. And ..."

"Totally out of your league?"

"Enough, Sadie." But she lifts her shoulder as if she agrees with my statement. "I didn't want to just drop this on you. Not until you had the opportunity to get to know him better."

"So that's the reason you subjected me to his class?"

"Well, I also hoped you would develop some level of confidence in your driving ability. Scott discovering how wonderful you are was a side benefit."

I throw my head back and laugh. "Total backfire, Mom. He thinks I'm an idiot."

"Why would he think that? Didn't he give you an A?"

"The A was for a written exam. But I tend to give off a strange vibe whenever I'm near mechanical objects. He might have witnessed an incident or two during the practical training portion of Driver's Ed."

Mom smiles and reaches out to tuck a stray lock of hair behind my ear. "Like mother, like daughter. Why do you think I walk to work?"

"You're not going to tell him that I know the truth, are you?"

"Do you want me to?"

"I really, really, really don't want you to tell him. At least not until some day, far in the future. When I can look him in the eye without remembering all the bizarre things I said because I thought in-class Driver's Ed was worthless."

Mom gasps. "You told Scott his class was worthless?"

"I never actually said worthless, but my attitude may have indicated something to that effect."

Mom sinks her head into her open hand. I can't tell if she's ready to laugh or cry.

"Hey, Mom," I whisper, and she lifts her eyes to mine, "He's not out of your league. Mr. Drum was lucky to find someone as great as you."

"Thank you, Sadie," she whispers back. I hug her tight, laying my head against her chest. When she pulls away, I see her wipe away a tear. And I know it's not going to be just the two of us for much longer.

***

After Mom and I spend the night talking about "Scott", I oversleep the next morning. I rush into homeroom just as the bell rings. With a stern look, Mrs. Warren hands me a folded sheet of paper.

Senior Superlative Digital Yearbook Photos Today. Bring Your Best Smile.

Geezus. I just started talking to Andy again, and now we're sitting for engagement pictures.

"Mrs. Downey is waiting for you, Sadie," Mrs. Warren says. "She's called twice."

I muss my hair with my hands as I run to the photo shoot, wishing I'd carried a tube of lipstick in my purse. By the time I arrive, Andy's already waiting for me. He looks so nervous, you'd think we were actually about to get married. For some reason, seeing his absolute terror makes me feel calmer. I smile brightly at him and touch his arm.

"Hey, Andy."

"S-S-Sadie," he stammers.

I rise onto my tiptoes and whisper in his ear. "Let's just have fun with this, okay?"

He nods stiffly and wraps his arm around my shoulder, drawing me closer, like I'm his security blanket. At Mrs. Downey's command, we pose in front of a big mural of pink hearts she keeps in her room for the Homecoming and Valentine's Day dances.

"Andy, lift her up, like you're carrying her over the threshold," Mrs. Downey suggests while half the A.V. club surrounds us, shooting video and snapping about a million photos. Could this experience be more painful? I'm about ready to puke up my breakfast. The rapid fire of camera flashes blinds me and now I'm freaking out as much as Andy. But he sweeps me into his arms, and suddenly his smile offers the encouragement I need. Like we both know this is all too ridiculous for words. I wrap my arms around his neck and gaze into his blue eyes, which are doing that happy twinkling thing I love, even as his sweaty palms drench the back of my shirt.

"You guys look so cute," says a squeaky voice. I startle and Andy grips me tighter.

"One more pose," Mrs. Downey says as Colette pops out from behind the cameraman. After Andy sets me down, she runs over to give us both hugs.

"You never mentioned anything about working on the yearbook committee, Colette," I say, as my eyes narrow.

"Oh, um, well, it was just something to do. In my free time." Now she's the one stammering nervously.

"See you in class, Sadie?" Andy asks, pausing at the door.

I wave to him. "See you later." As soon as he's gone, I turn back to Colette. "You fixed the vote, didn't you?" I hiss. "I just don't know why. Jealousy, maybe? Why would you want to humiliate me in front of the whole school?"

Tears spring to the corners of Colette's eyes. "I didn't do it to embarrass you, Sadie. It's just that," she says, wringing her hands, "Andy likes you a lot. He always has."

I take a step back, hoping her impending meltdown isn't contagious. "What? How do you know that?"

"I worked with him for a month last semester. We helped the middle school kids research a STEM career project. Anyway, I was totally in love with Andy. But, you're the only girl he ever talked about."

I shake my head. "You must have misread him. We barely even looked at each other last semester." Or the eleven years prior.

"No, *you* barely acknowledged *him*. But he tried to talk to you all the time. When he wasn't watching you. I know. Because I was watching him."

I want to argue my point, but I need to stop and think. Did I miss Andy's attention? Did all his annoying jokes and good-natured teasing serve a greater purpose?

"It can't be true," I say, more to myself.

"Oh, it's true," Colette says. "I fixed the Senior Superlative vote. Because you never saw him, not the way he wanted you to, and you're graduating soon, and I just think you guys would be so perfect together." Colette lets out a shaky breath and crosses her arms over her chest, as if prepared to shield herself should I decide to take a swing at her.

"Colette," I say. "When I saw my name on the bulletin board with Andy, I wanted to die. I mean, who does that? Who votes for a person to marry another person when they've never been on one date together? I thought someone was playing a joke on me. And because of that, I was extra mean to Andy, just to prove I didn't like him."

Colette blushes. "I know. My plan sorta backfired. But, it seems like you made up. Are you friends, at least?"

I nod. "Yes, we're friends. But it took us a long time to get there." The first bell rings and I gather my morning binders. "Tell me something, though. I know each person is only allowed one Senior Superlative Award. Was Andy supposed to be *Most Likely to Succeed*?"

Colette looks at her black boots. She doesn't need to tell me the answer. "He really likes you, Sadie. Plus, he got into MIT early admission, so he didn't need the other award."

"You need to tell him the truth."

Her eyes widen in fear. "But he may not take me to the freshman dance."

"You'll find another date. He deserves to know. And he should hear it from the person who fixed the vote."

As I turn to go, Colette calls out one final request. "Sadie? If you two get married, can I be your maid of honor?"

***

"Are you ready for this?" Jana asks. Together, we peek around the curtain on the opening night of *Little Shop of Horrors*. In the packed auditorium, the buzz of the crowd mixes with the jittery tension backstage, electrifying the atmosphere and setting off a high inside me unlike any I've ever experienced. Now I understand why people become addicted to performing.

I smooth my hands over my costume, a skin-tight green bodysuit dyed to blend in with the eight-foot tall plant designed by the robotics club. Thank goodness I'm an above average student, because all the buttons and levers on Audrey II have my head ready to explode.

"Do you know your lines?" I ask Jana. She'd been practicing while I'd changed into my plant outfit. Everyone, even Derek, pretty much knows their stuff at this point, thanks to the last week of nonstop rehearsals. Jana and I secretly believe Mrs. Bitty snuck some of her memory boosting vitamins into the water cooler in the choir room, because all of a sudden our mess of a show just clicked in everyone's heads. The entire cast bonded in a way I'd never expected, as if we'd survived a long, drawn out war together. Tonight is our victory party.

To encourage audience stragglers to take their seats, Mrs. Bitty launches the fanfare, her fingers plucking away at the piano as if a puppet master is pulling strings tied to her hands from above. The rest of her body remains eerily still, and after weeks of watching her perform, I would swear on my life that she's capable of simultaneously napping and playing show tunes. After a few discordant bars of the Little Shop theme song, the school orchestra joins in, the curtains swing open, and the first act begins.

Audrey II is hidden offstage for the first number, but I climb inside the shiny green metallic stem to hide from the rest of the cast when a sudden attack of stage fright hits me. My hands start to shake and my breathing turns shallow. Through a peep hole in the middle of the huge plant contraption, I glimpse my mother sitting in the front row and instantly feel calmer.

Next to Mom sits Aunt Tina, who left work early, rode the Acela train into Philly from New York, and then hopped on the regional rail line to Harmony. She threw open the door and strolled into our apartment, as if she'd only traveled a few blocks from her office. Aunt Tina was a member of the Harmony High drama club before succumbing to art of leveraged buyouts, so she's beyond thrilled to watch me star in a musical at her former high school.

Before I'm completely ready, the crew rolls Audrey II on stage for our first scene, halfway through Act I. When the curtains rise, I twist my neck and raise my arm to adjust a branch. Audrey II's giant stem shifts a bit and through my peep hole I spot the person sitting on the opposite side of my mother.

Mr. Drum.

His tattooed arm rests on top of Mom's shoulders. At the sight, my knees cave in, and the plant sways precariously, forcing me to redirect my attention before the structure capsizes.

"Shoot!" I hiss, tightening my hold on the interior handles, straining to keep the thing upright.

"Sadie! Control Audrey II!" Mrs. Cutler stage-whispers from behind the curtain. I suck in a huge breath, lock my knees, ignore the ache in my hamstring, and attempt to get back into character.

As they say in the acting business, the show must go on, despite the shocking appearance of my mother's new love interest, who also happens to be my ex-Driver's Ed instructor. I manipulate Audrey II like a pro, and my timing even draws several big laughs from the audience. Jana's growling Audrey II voice wavers a bit for the first scene. After we receive our first round of applause, she suddenly snaps into character. By the end of Act II, I don't even mind my striking resemblance to a sequined, glittery pea pod.

As we take our formal bows, I step out from behind an immense leaf and wave to the roaring crowd. Ten rows back, Andy's head pokes up above the masses. When our eyes meet, he brings two fingers to his mouth and whistles long and loud, inciting further applause. Mr. Drum follows suit and a huge grin spreads over my face. I soak up the audience's thundering appreciation until the curtain drops like a ton of bricks, abruptly ending my big moment.

"Was that who I think it was clapping for you?" Jana asks as she helps unravel me from a gauzy outer layer of glittery leaves.

"Who, Mr. Drum?"

"Mr. Drum was in the audience? I meant Andy. Chica, I think you need to set some relationship parameters before you invite everyone to see you in action."

"I didn't invite either of them. They just showed up!" I dig my green-painted fingernails into her arm. "Don't let me go out there alone."

"Ha! I wouldn't miss this for all the sequins on your sparkly, green leotard."

Together, we walk into the darkened, mostly empty auditorium.

"No Andy in sight," Jana whispers. "Conflict avoided. Good luck with Mr. D." Like a coward, she slips out the side door to find Ben, leaving me alone to deal with my family drama.

"You were wonderful," Mom says, grinning broadly when I join their little group.

"Stunning. I truly believed you were a plant," Aunt Tina agrees. "Right, Scott?"

"Nice job, kid," Mr. Drum says, shifting his hulking weight back and forth. Do teachers get nervous in front of students, ever? I guess when they've been kissing your mother, they do.

"What a fun night this has been," Aunt Tina says, with a sly smile. "Scott, I hear you taught our little Sadie here how to drive."

"Just the classroom portion, Aunt Tina," I say. "I'm not driving yet."

"After I finish helping Kathleen brush up on her driving skills, Sadie, maybe we can go out together." Mr. Drum turns to Mom. "You're the most beautiful driving student I've ever had. But also, the least mechanically inclined."

"Really? As bad as me?" I ask.

"Worse," he says. He's dead serious.

"Maybe your teaching skills are the problem. Right, Sadie?" Mom asks, but she's looking at Mr. Drum. Her hand rests on his forearm, covering one of his scarier tattoos.

"I refuse to answer any teacher-related questions until after graduation," I say. Meanwhile, Mr. Drum leans in and kisses Mom right on the lips. Oh, yuck! Aunt Tina and I engage in mutual eye rolling.

"Can I talk the three of you into a late dinner at The Green Lagoon?" Mr. Drum asks after he and Mom break it off.

I'd prefer the floor to open up and swallow me whole rather than sit through an entire meal with my Driver's Ed teacher. But, given my mom's current state of rapture, I'm okay with risking total embarrassment for the sake of her happiness.

Plus, The Green Lagoon has excellent burgers.

***

Mom and Aunt Tina sit through the entire *Little Shop* show again on Saturday night, along with my mother's now official significant other. Meaning that we are all now aware they are a couple, but we still need to work out a few kinks in our family dynamic. Treating me to a burger at The Green Lagoon was a smart way to begin a long, mutually appreciative relationship, though. Everyone loosens up after a few green beers (or in my case, diet Cokes) and the four of us really bond. Mr. Drum didn't reveal my driving distractions list, for which I will owe him for all of eternity. Aunt Tina and my mother bickered about their clothes and hair like sisters do, and we all laughed about my Audrey II costume.

After dinner, Mr. Drum dropped Aunt Tina off at the train station before driving Mom and me home in his truck. He told us how he rebuilt the engine, which he claimed purred like a kitten. Mom pretended to be interested, and I closed my eyes in the back seat as the exhausting schedule I'd kept the last few months finally caught up with me.

At the end of the night, Mom invited Mr. Drum into our apartment. I can't say this for sure, but when I entered my room, ready to collapse into twelve hours of deep sleep, he didn't appear to be in a hurry to leave.

I'm just glad he didn't stick around for breakfast. I doubt Mr. Drum would even recognize me sans makeup. Morning-after Sadie is not a pretty sight.

Anyway, I miss a few cues during the second Little Shop show because I'm so happy and excited for Mom. I know Mr. Drum, and deep down, he is a good person. For years, I feared my mother would end up with a total rat. No one, and I mean no one, wants rat relatives, even if they are step-relatives.

When the last notes of the finale echo in the air, the

curtain drops and the audience roars. The stage crew yanks the curtain back up, and I notice Andy, much closer to the stage tonight, clapping with his hands held above his head. Our eyes meet, and then he jogs up to the stage with a huge bouquet of flowers. Jana is squealing next to me, because Ben gave her flowers too.

But mine are bigger. Just saying.

I stare at Andy, completely speechless, but he just shrugs as if to say, it's all cool and walks back to his family. All of the Super Ks are in attendance for my last-ever performance as a plant.

Should I have kissed Andy, like Jana kissed Ben? In front of everyone? I flash back to my last kiss with Andy and remember how much trouble I had stopping the process once we got started. No way is that happening with both of our mothers less than ten feet away.

Next up is the cast party at Leslie's house. I hurry backstage; tearing off pieces of my costume, ready to kiss the green monstrosity good-bye. The stage crew lumps together near the exit, wearing black T-shirts, acting too cool to mingle with the cast, but Leslie told me they always show up for free food. Jana holds both of our flowers while I shed my final layer of glittery gauze.

"Ben's waiting for me," she says.

"Will he go to the cast party?"

"I'm not sure. We may have other plans. Why don't

you walk out with us?" Jana says, acting oddly evasive.

In the parking lot, we run into Andy and Sidh, talking with a group of younger girls, including Colette. And Melinda Banner. I stare hard at Jana's little sister, and she nods her head, sending me an affirmation, before looking away with sad eyes.

"Ben's over there. Be right back." Jana takes off toward her boyfriend's minivan, deserting me among the sea of girls circling Andy and Sidh.

"Nice flowers. Apparently there was some truth to the Senior Superlative." Melinda sashays over to me.

Rather than disagree, I clench my jaw shut. Though I'll never admit it, Melinda's probably right. Colette uncovered the truth I hadn't been able to find on my own. I place my hand on my hip and lift my chin in defiance. "Who knows the truth? You might have missed the story of the year at Harmony High."

Melinda's nose wrinkles. "Andy and Sadie the story of the year? I think not." She spins around and huffs off.

"Sore loser," I mutter.

"Great job, Sadie," Sidh says, reaching out to punch my arm affectionately.

"Thanks. Did Andy pay you to come with him tonight?"

"Nah. He mentioned something about you manipulating mechanical devices while dressed in skimpy clothes." Sidh's thick eyebrows wiggle up and down suggestively. Andy leans back against his car; a guilty grin plastered on his face. Slowly, the group of girls begins to drift away.

"Thanks for the flowers," I say, turning to Andy.

"No problem. It's a closing night tradition. That's what I heard, anyway."

I wonder who gives him his information.

"So, no tutoring tonight?" I ask.

He smiles. "Nope. Some of us are going to Bella Pizza. If you want to come, I'll drop you off at Leslie's later. I hear the cast party is an all-night event."

Again with the inside info.

"Um, let me check with Jana. I'm not sure ..." I say, and dash over to my best friend, standing with Ben next to Dominic's car.

"What's up, sis?" Dom asks. We share a smile. Dom would make a great brother. As far as his boyfriend potential, well, he needs to work on that.

"Are we doing the party thing, Jana?" I ask.

"Dom and Ben want to grab pizza first. The van's low on gas, so Dom's driving. I don't think you can fit." Jana grins triumphantly and then slides her gaze across the parking lot to Andy.

"Plant-girl can sit on my lap." Dominic smirks.

"You know what, I think Sidh and Andy are going

to Bella Pizza too. I can just catch a ride with them and meet you there, okay?"

"Great idea, Sadie," Jana says with a sweetly innocent smile.

My best friend is on the brink of achieving her dream ride in the Altomeri hot rod.

"Are you jealous?" she asks, lowering herself onto Ben's lap. His arms wrap around her like a safety belt.

"Not at all. Add it to our list," I say. "See you when I see you."

"Have fun riding with Andy," she calls, as they zoom away.

By the time I return to Andy, he's all alone. "Where's Sidh?"

"Previous engagement. Ready to go?"

I sweep my eyes around the empty parking lot. "With you?"

Andy's light eyebrows raise. "Do you have another ride?"

"No, but … just the two of us?"

"Something wrong with that?"

"No, I, uh …"

"Sadie, I trusted you enough to let you drive my car. Don't you trust me?" Andy's blue eyes gleam in the moonlight, daring me to say no.

This is what I wanted, right? I think so. I climb into

the passenger's side.

"Did you talk to Colette?" I ask him once I'm settled.

He nods. "You were right. The vote was fixed."

"Andy, I'm sorry you didn't get the *Most Likely to Succeed* award. It's the one Senior Superlative that actually matters." I fold my hands in my lap and twist my fingers together tightly.

But, Andy, being Andy, doesn't appear upset. "Cindy Min deserves it, too. She's already written like three novels or something. Besides, Colette's right, I'd already gotten into my first choice for college."

"Well, not that it means anything, but I voted for you as *Most Likely to Succeed*."

Andy presses the power button on the dash to start his car. "It means a lot. Thanks. So, you and Mr. Drum, huh?" he asks, trying to be causal, but I hear a hitch in his voice.

I burst out laughing. "Ugh. No way."

"Really? He looked a little overly affectionate when he hugged you after the show last night. For a Driver's Ed teacher, that is." After checking the rear view mirror, Andy backs out of the parking spot. "You and Jana always talk about how Mr. Drum's so good-looking. But he's, like old enough to be your dad ..." Andy clears his throat and pauses, at a loss. I decide to help him out.

"That's a good thing, because he's dating my mom."

Andy screeches to a stop in the middle of a three point turn, narrowly missing the dumpster sitting beside the cafeteria.

"Watch it! Do you want to get us killed?" I scream.

"No. Sorry. Can you say that again?"

"Mr. Drum has been secretly dating my mom. For five months. Some kind of forbidden love, I guess."

"And no one told you?"

"No! I just found out. My mom made me take Driver's Ed because she was hoping I would realize he's a great guy before she fessed up. But I was kind of clueless."

"Well, who expects that to be the underlying reason for mandated driving instruction?" Andy shakes his head in wonder. "Are you okay with their, uh, relationship?"

"Yeah, sure. I mean, it was sort of a shock, but now … I'm okay."

"Good. I guess. Sorry, but I don't even know what to say, Sadie."

"It's fine, Andy. I'm still adjusting to it myself."

We drive on in silence.

"So, do you get to keep the costume?" he asks.

"The bejeweled green leotard? Yes. You can borrow it, but I don't think it will fit you."

"Heh heh heh."

At the sound of Andy's laugh, the tension between us dissolves. I crack up. Seriously. I cannot stop laughing.

"Hey. What?" he asks, reaching for my hand to stop it from repeatedly banging his dashboard. His fingers curl around mine and I freeze mid-slap. "Did you spend too much time squeezed into the plant?"

"No. I'm fine. Good." I take a minute to steady myself, pretending to be interested in the view of the Harmony passing by, so familiar that I'm sure in the past seventeen plus years I'd memorized every house on every street. If someone repaints their shutters, I trust myself to pick up on the difference.

High above, the night sky seems to float down to earth, wrapping around me like a blanket. A bright yellow moon hangs low, grazing the roof of the courthouse. Andy makes me happy, I realize. I just like being with him. And, I feel like I can tell him anything, and he would at least try to understand. Which is more than most other guys my age would do.

"You know, we've been friends for a long time," I say.

"I wouldn't categorize our relationship as friendship, exactly," he responds, thoughtfully.

"Okay, we've known each other for years."

"But not really well."

"Andy, am I missing something I should know about my alleged future husband? Are you a closet cross-dresser? Is that why you want my costume?" I squeeze my fingers tighter to let him know I'm joking, and he squeezes back.

"Nothing like that," he says. "I just think it would be nice if we learned more about each other. Especially if the Senior Superlative turns out to be a reliable predictor of the future and we do wind up getting married. For example, you know my family and you know about my goal of learning to fly. I know you have a ridiculous list of achievements you feel the need to complete before graduation."

"So, we're about even, then."

Andy heh-hehs. "Not quite."

"What do you want to me to tell you?"

"Anything. You're great at avoiding serious conversation, you know."

I do know. It's not by accident that I refrain from telling people about my boring life.

"My name is Sadie Elizabeth Matthews," I begin. Andy nods, a sign of encouragement. "I live with my mom in the Cambridge House apartments. And I was recently introduced to her new boyfriend, who happens to be my ex-Driver's Ed instructor."

"Sounds like you have some future sitcom potential. I talked to your mother after the show, by the way. She's really proud of you."

"You talked to my mom?"

"And your aunt. She's nice too. Kind of like an older version of you."

My mouth drops open, and my chin just about hits the dashboard. "Why? Why did you talk to them?"

Andy sighs, as if he's being forced to communicate with a very naïve young child.

"Because I'm a nice guy, Sadie. And because I want you to like me as much as I like you."

I hinge my jaw closed and open again. A million different words run through my mind, but I can't say any of them. So, I blurt out the one question I've wanted to ask for weeks now.

"Will you go to the prom with me, Andrew?"

Fill It In – Random List
The Top Ten Reasons Why Andy is an Awesome Prom Date.

1. He's a really good kisser.
2. Just looking into his blue eyes makes me smile.
3. He's known me forever, so I don't have to impress him. But, I know he'll still appreciate how nice I look in my prom dress.
4. He makes me laugh.
5. Besides Mr. Drum (Scott), who faced death on a daily basis for years as an Army Ranger, Andy is the only person brave enough to get into the car when I'm behind the wheel. Although, he says he's more afraid of driving with me than solo flying an airplane. I'm pretty sure he's joking.
6. His car is small, so I don't have to reach very far when I want to kiss him. Which is frequently.
7. He thinks Chase is an excellent boy's name.
8. He's super tall, so I can wear those ridiculous heels I bought at the Macy's One Day Sale and I still probably won't make it above his shoulder.
9. He asked what color prom dress I picked, and he actually listened to the answer. Then, when I quizzed him an hour later, he remembered what I said.
10. He's the best man. And he loves me.

Chapter Twenty-Three

Mrs. McCaffrey was right. It's better to hold out.

On prom night, Mr. Drum, I mean Scott, as he keeps insisting I call him, opens the door to greet my date. Scott has assumed the duty of potential step-father and he does his best to scare Andy while Mom helps me finish my make-up.

My grand entrance entails simply walking out of my bedroom and past the dining table. Four giant steps later, I reach Andy, who's grinning and holding flowers. Andy just fills up space well, especially when formally attired in a classic black tux, with his hair combed and cut a few inches shorter than the last time I saw him.

Ah, the miracles of hair gel.

Not that I don't appreciate his messy look as well. In the last month, since he agreed to be my date, I've discovered that I like everything about Andrew Kosolowski.

We stand smiling at each other like a pair of deranged lovebirds, completely forgetting our audience. My heartbeat goes all screwy and I forget to breathe until Andy clears his throat and it hits me that Mr. Drum, I mean Scott, (I'll get it right one of these days), looks as if he wants to test out some new para-military weapons on the guy who is brave enough to escort me to the prom.

Andy hands me the bright pink roses he picked out, which perfectly match my dress. Mom wipes a tear from her eye, and Scott (Mr. Drum) kisses me on the cheek. My heart feels swollen, brimming over with love and happiness, and I pray to high heaven that my Spanx will hold everything in place before something inside of me explodes.

***

"So, the last time I saw that achievement list, there were a few empty spots at the bottom," Andy says as we drive to the prom. Of course, I'd offered to drive, as I am more than ready to break in my brand-new license, but he insisted on getting behind the wheel. Admittedly, hitting the brakes while sporting four-inch heels is a challenge, even for a driver with more than two days' experience, but I was willing to try.

"Earth to Sadie," he prompts. Andy has a way of knocking the words right out of my head. "I'm offering my assistance to help you fill it in. Do you want to cut out of the prom and go to the zoo? Photo bomb the president? Rob a bank, maybe?"

I smile coyly and gaze at him from under my falsely extended eyelashes. "Jana and Ben are swinging by school on the way to the prom for some PDA in front of the school sign. After that, we just need one more achievement. Robbing a bank is a good suggestion. I was thinking about breaking a law, but I wasn't going to aim as high as a felony."

Falling in love, the one achievement I truly doubted would be possible, is happening everywhere. Jana and Ben. Andy and me. Dominic and himself. Even my mother and Mr. Drum checked off that particular item on their list of amazing lifetime achievements. They're planning a wedding this summer. Before Andy and I leave for college. I'm not attending MIT, but in the last two months I've pretty much applied to every school in a thirty-mile radius.

"Sadie, you've already broken a law. Repeatedly."

"I have? I mean, sure, you're a few months younger

than me, but really, no one gets arrested for statutory kissing, do they?"

"Not the kissing," Andy says, with a laugh. "I let you drive my car, remember? Before your permit test."

"Driving without a permit? That counts?"

Andy smiles down at me. "Sure does."

"Would I be arrested or fined?"

"A police officer would issue you a written citation, and you wouldn't be allowed to take the license test until you turn eighteen. I looked it up after I let you drive my car in the Towne Center parking lot. Did you have any other last-minute, unachieved high school aspirations besides breaking a law?"

I shake my head, but not too fast, because I don't want to mess up my hair. "No."

"Then you're good. Can we still meet Ben and Jana in front of the sign? I want my name penciled next to as many list items as possible."

"The list is what brought us together."

"You credit the list, not Colette, who fixed the Senior Superlative vote or our previous twelve years of mutual respect and admiration?"

"Huh?"

"Sorry. Too many words?"

"It's prom night, Andy. Can we cool it with the nerd talk for a few hours?"

"Only if you're prepared to publicly proclaim your affection."

"Sure, whatever. Let's do it," I agree. I text Jana to let her know about our change in plans. We pull up in front of school just as the fiery sun sinks behind the building, pulling what's left of daylight below the horizon.

"We're finishing this with two weeks to spare," I announce, removing the dog-eared, crumpled paper from Aunt Tina's silver evening bag.

"Yeah, now the real slacking off begins," Jana says. "Total senioritis. Do you want to go first?"

"Let's do it together. All four of us," I say.

"I'm not kissing Kosolowski," Ben insists.

"Only me, baby," Jana promises, attaching herself to his lips.

While the two of them are otherwise occupied, I stretch up on my tiptoes and circle my arms around Andy's neck. A prom-bound car filled with our friends passes by and honks. Andy tenses his shoulders and starts to pull back. I lock my arms around him and kiss him as if letting go would mean the end of humanity as we know it. When my knees start to buckle, he lifts me in his arms.

"Reputation ruined," he says, with a wicked grin.

"This was your suggestion," I remind him and press my lips to his once more. "Besides, the only way to prove your love is real is to kiss me twice."

Fill It In – Your Awesome Achievements

1. Break a School Rule – Sadie & Jana Cut Homeroom!
2. Serve My First Detention - Sadie
3. Star in the School Play – Sadie & Jana are Audrey II
4. Pass Driver's Ed – Sadie & Jana
5. ~~Kiss Two Boys in One Night - Sadie~~
6. Ride in Dominic Altomeri's Stingray — Jana
7. Break a Law – Sadie Drives Without a Permit
8. Score a Varsity Letter – Mathletes Champs! (Mostly thanks to Andy)
9. Convince Mr. Drum to get into a car with you — Sadie
10. Kiss Shy Ben In Public — Jana
11. Fall in Love — Jana & Ben, Sadie & Andy

ACKNOWLEDGEMENTS

Writing has always made me happy. When I decided to seriously try to write a book, I never expected to meet so many readers and writers who would be willing to offer advice or read my work. Thanks to everyone who supported me.

Specifically, I need to thank an amazing writer and friend, Theresa Hernandez, for sticking with this story from beginning to end and every iteration in between. Your feedback and encouragement kept me going through the many ups and downs of the writing process. Sadie & Jana wouldn't exist without you.

Thanks to my friend Audrey for reading and loving everything I write. Everyone needs an Audrey in their life. And thanks to the other many writers, readers, critique partners, friends, and relatives who also contributed to my story. Special thanks to Karole, Sally, Natalia, Carrie, and Dawn for reading and critiquing. Also thanks to my Philly critique group for helping me with my final round of revisions. Thanks to Pat Calvert, my teacher. I needed honest feedback and you gave it to me with gusto. I still hear you in my head reminding me to loosen up my dialogue.

I also want to thank Mom and Dad for turning off the television and encouraging us to read. To my sisters

Amy and Maria and my brothers, Gerard and Nick, thanks for letting me bounce ideas off you and for always being willing to talk about books. And thanks to my sister-in-laws Eileen and Genevieve, for offering their expert advice and unwavering support.

Thanks to my husband Dean for not laughing too hard when I told him I was giving up my business career to be a writer. Also, for making the adjustments we needed to make to help my dream come true. A shout out goes to my kids, Dean, Matthew, and Kristen for always insisting I'm the best writer in the world.

I'd also like to send my appreciation to the Hernandez kids, Mattea, Noah, and Grayson, for supplying the teen feedback this book needed and helping me come up with a cool title.

Thanks to my Sixteen to Read debut author friends. Sharing this experience with you has been wonderfully uplifting. I'm eternally grateful for your support and encouragement.

Thanks to everyone at Georgia McBride Media Group for their input and advice. You made my book better with each suggestion and correction. And finally, thanks to Georgia McBride for emailing me at midnight to tell me she wanted me to publish my book. Yes, I was awake, and it was one of the most fun emails I've ever gotten. Thanks for supporting so many yet-to-be published writers.

JENNIFER DIGIOVANNI

Jennifer is a freelance writer and YA author. When she's not writing, you can find her reading, working on home design projects, or trying to meet her daily goals on her Fitbit. *My Senior Year of Awesome* is her first novel.

OTHER SWOON ROMANCE TITLES YOU MIGHT LIKE

RIVAL DREAMS
LIFE IN THE NO-DATING ZONE
EFFORTLESS WITH YOU

Find more awesome teen romance books at http://www. myswoonromance.com/

Connect with Swoon Romance online:

Facebook: www.Facebook.com/swoonromance
Twitter: https://twitter.com/SwoonRomance
You Tube: https://www.youtube.com/swoonromance
Instagram: https://instagram.com/swoonromance/
Request review copies via swoonromancepr@gmail.com

NATALIE DECKER

Rival Dreams

—— 💜 ——

Their Rules. Game On.

LIFE in the
no-dating ZONE

Patricia B. Tighe

EFFORTLESS *with* YOU

A NOVEL

LIZZY CHARLES